Undercover Princess

Undercover Princess

A Castles of Dallas Romance

Lenora Worth

TULE
PUBLISHING

Undercover Princess
Copyright © 2018 Lenora Worth
Tule Publishing First Printing, January 2018

The Tule Publishing Group, LLC

ALL RIGHTS RESERVED

First Publication by Tule Publishing Group 2018

Second Edition

No part of this book may be used or reproduced in any manner whatsoever without written permission except in the case of brief quotations embodied in critical articles and reviews.

This is a work of fiction. Names, characters, places, and incidents are products of the author's imagination or are used fictitiously. Any resemblance to actual events, locales, organizations, or persons, living or dead, is entirely coincidental.

ISBN: 978-1-948342-41-4

Chapter One

"I DON'T THINK I can do this."

Eleanor Castle stared at her image in the full-length mirror, the muted light from the gleaming chandelier reminding her that she didn't belong here. The red sleeveless cocktail dress with the broad portrait collar was elegant on her. She'd lost close to twenty pounds since the last time she'd stood in this spot over fourteen years ago, and the dress fit her body like a glove. Cinching at her tiny waist, the flared skirt belled out in chiffon brilliance, giving her figure an hourglass shape. The result was a nod to Valentine's Day, sexy while still being classy.

"You're gonna be just fine," Tiffany Jackson, a friend who worked downstairs in the cosmetic department of the famous Dallas flagship Castle Department Store, said to reassure her.

Tiffany fussed over the gleaming diamond necklace and matching teardrop earrings she'd borrowed from the jewelry department. "If you can get through tonight, we'll have a real Valentine's Day celebration in two weeks, on the real day."

Eleanor couldn't believe her bad timing. Her new position started on the same week Castle Department Store planned to begin its centennial celebration. The original

Castle's had opened two weeks before Valentine's Day in 1918.

The theme for this year's celebration was *One Hundred Years of Elegance and Grace*.

And once upon a time, she'd been part of that elegance and grace.

"But what if someone recognizes me?" Eleanor said, her gaze moving over the elegant chignon Tiffany had insisted on creating in spite of Eleanor's unruly hair. The hairstyle showed off her newly highlighted blonde curls, while making her look like a princess from a fairy tale. Tiffany's talent for doing a makeover was impressive, but had Eleanor changed enough to fool everyone? "I know I look different now, but—"

"Honey, hush," Tiffany said, waving a hand in dismissal, her purple-lacquered fingernails sparkling. "I almost didn't recognize you when you showed up on my doorstep a month ago. You've changed, Miss Eleanor Castle."

"Shh," Eleanor said, glancing around to make sure they were alone. It was necessary, however, since they were in a private dressing room on the top floor of the six-story building. "No one can know who I really am. Not yet, anyway. Only you and my father ever called me Ellie and he only called me that when my mother was alive. So out in the store and around others, I'm Ellie Sheridan."

Her father had become more formal after his new wife came into their home.

Tiffany ran a hand over her inky braids, her burnished brown eyes as bright as the single solitaire she wore with her wedding band on her left ring finger. Eleanor's childhood friend had married a good man and had four beautiful children, but Tiffany still enjoyed a good conspiracy and loved being in on a covert mission.

"Your secret is safe with me," she said on a quiet note. "And Claude never tells any of our secrets, even though he could write a book on the goings-on around this place."

That was true. If memory served Eleanor, the wise maintenance man played Santa each Christmas and handed out silly handmade heart-shaped cards each Valentine's Day, and never said a bad thing about anyone. He remembered everyone's birthday, and he knew who was out sick and usually made them homemade chicken soup. And he loved playing matchmaker, or at least he had when Eleanor used to roam around the store.

"I hope he'll keep my secret," Eleanor said. "Because I need you both to be my eyes and ears if I'm going to pull this off."

She didn't tell her dear friend she'd already set things in motion by hiring lawyers and doing tons of research online. She needed to build a compelling case against her stepmother. And possibly press charges against the ruthless woman who had taken over Castle's and ruined Eleanor's life years ago.

Tiffany finished with a flourish, touching up Eleanor's cheeks with glittery blush. "You can start your job as head of security bright and early Monday morning, but tonight, you are my plus one for this Valentine's Gala, so enjoy it and do all the spying you want. Castle's is throwing a big party this year with this centennial celebration stuff. No one will recognize you because they'll be too busy drinking champagne and eating those fancy appetizers the café whipped up."

Eleanor turned from the mirror, the sweeping skirt of her dress making her feel special again. She'd felt that way long ago, when she'd been the princess of Castle Department Store, walking down the grand staircase with her parents holding her hands on either side, loving every minute of their annual Valentine's Gala, which had always been held close to *the* big day—her birthday.

Back then, her parents always made a big deal about holidays. They'd celebrated Thanksgiving by volunteering so others would have a good meal, Christmas with an open house for customers and workers alike, and Memorial Day and the Fourth of July with fireworks. Any holiday was cause for celebration at Castle's, and not just for sales or profits. Her parents had truly loved their employees like family. But Valentine's Day had always been Eleanor's favorite because her parents loved throwing this elaborate gala as a special birthday event for her, as well as an anniversary event for the store.

Charles and Vivian Castle had been known around Dallas/Ft Worth for their charitable donations and their generosity to employees. Lately, however, Castle Department Store had been slipping in those endeavors. Employee morale was down, and they'd lost some of their best people. Plus, customers were leaving unsavory comments and reviews on the website. At least funds from tonight's big event would go to a local organization that helped place women back into the working world. But only because the head of the House of Lamon, who was at the center of this publicity, had demanded it.

Caron Castle, her stepmother, didn't care about anyone but herself.

Which was why Eleanor Castle, the true heir to the Castle fortune, was back. Eleanor could live without the fortune, but she wouldn't let her father's legacy go down in flames simply because the woman in charge didn't have a clue about managing a vast department store conglomerate. Besides this flagship store, there were several more stores located across the South. Her father, who'd always been at the helm, hadn't been seen in public for months now. All the more reason for Eleanor to return, no matter the timing.

It was now or never. She had to discover what was wrong with her father, and she had to find a way to bring Caron Castle down from her high-and-mighty throne.

When Eleanor was fifteen, her mother had died. A year later, her grieving father had married the first gold digger to come along. And she'd brought two younger children with her and later talked Eleanor's father into officially adopting them.

Shocked and confused, Eleanor had rebelled and acted out in every conceivable way for the next few years.

The princess had been relegated to the far tower. Her once-doting father had suddenly forgotten she existed, except for the times he called her into his office to lecture her on her rude behavior toward his new wife. So Eleanor Castle had gone off to college. Brokenhearted and devastated, she'd still managed to graduate with degrees in both business and criminal justice. She'd landed a job in security at a major retail store similar to Castles, but located in faraway Atlanta. Biding her time, she'd waited for an opening in the Atlanta Castle's store in hope of getting a position here.

In all that time, her father had never reached out to her or responded to her letters or phone calls. She blamed Caron for that.

But now, Ellie Sheridan, aka Eleanor Castle, had come home to reclaim what rightly belonged to her. But it wasn't about money or material things. No, Eleanor had a better reason for being back.

"What made you decide to come back now?" Tiffany asked, handing Eleanor her a pair of exquisite shimmering silver leather pumps. Eleanor's friend had always been able to decipher her thoughts. "You've been gone for almost fourteen years."

Eleanor slid one shoe on and moaned. "You know why. Let me enjoy this moment. I've been gone, and I've changed. At least I shed those college pounds."

Her friend let out an unladylike snort. "You did more than lose a few pounds. You're in great shape, and your hair is gorgeous. You're not the same shy, mousy teenager who left here."

"I've changed in other ways, too," Eleanor said, remembering what a mess she'd been when she'd gone off to college. "I actually love pretty shoes now."

"They're Lamon's," Tiffany said with a grin and a fluttering of her hands. "Like walking on heaven. Louboutin and Manolo have nothing on Lamon."

Eleanor took in a breath. "And so expensive I can't even begin to keep them." She knew because she'd splurged on shoes a few times, most of them hidden in her closet like secret trophies.

"They're yours," Tiffany said. "I do have an employee discount. Claude threw in a few bucks, too. Your welcome-home present."

"I can't," Eleanor said. But she stood and stared at her feet before twirling and admiring the stunning shoes. "Well, they do look good with this dress."

"Yes, they sure do," Tiffany said, clapping her hands. "I have to get downstairs. Monday, you can go back to being Plain Jane Eleanor. Your words, not mine—for the record. But tonight, you can be the princess at the ball. You'll even get to rub shoulders with none other than Nico Lamon himself."

Eleanor let out a snort. "Nico Lamon is a playboy who inherited a well-established Italian fashion house. He runs in circles that are so out of my league he won't even bat an eye toward me. I doubt the man will notice me since I only saw him once when I was a teenager when he was here with his parents. We were supposed to be forced together in publicity photos, but I got shoved aside so my stepsiblings could have the limelight. I never even got to introduce myself."

Because somehow, she'd managed to *accidentally* lock herself in her room. Eleanor had tried to call down for help, but no one answered the house phone. She'd banged on the door, hoping someone would come by. No one did.

Her bedroom door had never jammed like that before.

Memories of that awkward time when she'd missed a chance to see Nico at an afternoon tea assaulted her. Eleanor remembered Caron had fussed at her, saying her dress was too tight, her skin too pimply. Mortified, though she liked the rich blue dress she'd picked out and she only had one tiny pimple, Eleanor had stiffened her spine after Caron left her room. Her parents had taught her manners.

She had decided to hold her head high and ignore Caron's taunts. Whether Nico noticed her or not, she hadn't cared. She'd show her face and stand tall.

But she never had that chance.

She'd stood at her bedroom window, watching as his parents and their entourage loaded up in the limousine to leave.

And there he'd been, standing in the drive below.

Nico had looked like a cover model for GQ. Dark wavy hair and even darker midnight eyes. Perfect teeth and skin.

She'd looked down.

He'd glanced up.

Their gazes had held for a brief breath or two.

But then, he was gone.

Eleanor hated that even now, she still had a crush on the man. She'd dated and tried to find love, but her heart wasn't in it. She'd locked it up in a secret place. The boy she'd once had a crush on was now a man—an attractive thirty-five-year-old—and since he was in her castle, her treacherous heart was trying to escape.

"He's going to be too busy trying to find the perfect woman to wear those perfect Valentine's shoes he designed just for tonight to look at anyone like me, anyway." Shrugging, she added, "And from what I read in the tabloids, I'm not his type. He dates supermodels and movie stars."

"Well, you can still flirt with the man," Tiffany suggested with a wag of her finger. "I gotta get going. Caron will be on the war path if the employees aren't in their positions when we open the doors to those rich patrons who paid a pretty penny to be here."

"What if she recognizes me?" Eleanor asked, doubt coloring her words. Why she was nervous now, after she'd watched, waited, and worked so hard until the perfect opportunity came along, baffled her. She couldn't lose confidence in her plan.

Tiffany giggled. "Caron? No way. I barely recognized you. Besides, she'll be occupied with what she does best—bossing everyone around and making sure she's the center of attention. She has no idea who you are. Your paperwork went to HR, and she signed off on it without even reading it. She won't bother with you when you start working here. She's just worried about the rash of shoplifters we've had lately. Worried enough to fire our head of security and put out feelers for the best of the best. And you, my dear, have the best qualifications out of everyone who applied for the job."

"I did get my new position fair and square, as Ellie Sheridan," Eleanor said, proud of that. "Not like some people who are in charge around here."

Her stepmother and two stepsiblings came to mind. They were on salary, but from what Eleanor had heard, they didn't work at Castle's that much.

Tiffany grinned before heading for the secret side door that only a few employees knew about. They also didn't know about the now-empty apartment up here, but Eleanor planned to explore that when she had a chance.

"When we get home tonight," her friend said on a dramatic whirl, "I want the whole story of what you've been up to all these years, you hear me?"

"I left for all the wrong reasons," Eleanor replied, grit in each word. "But I have only one reason to return to Castle's. My father needs me."

Chapter Two

NICO SPOTTED HER the minute his security team cleared the way. A golden-haired woman in red was centered on the magnificent staircase, one hand on the rail and the other touching the exquisite diamond necklace at her throat.

He gazed up.

She looked down. At him.

Her gaze held an intensity that spoke of power, the jewels around her neck winking at him. Nico had a jolt of memory, like a feather brushing across his mind, but then it was gone.

"Mr. Lamon, I'm Caron Castle. Welcome."

Flicking a quick glance at the petite older woman with the brassy red bob of hair who'd positioned herself in his path, Nico noticed the dainty jewel-encrusted hand she extended. "Thank you, Mrs. Castle. It's a pleasure to be here."

The woman on the stairs moved, stepping down, her gaze leaving him to do a scan of the entire first floor of the huge department store. Was she searching for someone? Her date, maybe?

The thought disappointed Nico. But then, he rarely had time to date anyone. However, if she was single, he'd be willing to make the effort. She was exquisite.

"We're ready whenever you are," Caron Castle said, motioning to the employees gathered around to assist the crush of elite shoppers. "As you can see, a lot of young women are lined up and ready to try on these shoes, my daughter Annabelle among them. She does part-time modeling for us. She also works in the accessories department since she finished college a couple of years ago, so she'd be highly qualified for the position of spokesperson for Lamon footwear."

Caron tugged at the arm of a dark-haired beauty dressed in a black velvet gown with shards of green and blue sequins tossed onto the fabric liked spilled paint. "Annabelle, this is Nico Lamon."

"Mother, honestly," Annabelle said, rolling her kohl-heavy eyes. "You know I'm with Mick now."

She tugged a skinny-jeaned man with spiked blond hair toward them, letting her gaze flicker over Nico. "I'll try the shoes, though. I mean, they are Lamon. Who wouldn't want to try them on?"

Nico stared at the line of beautiful women who'd gone overboard with the hair and makeup tonight. This was Texas, after all, where everything was big, brash, and over the top. Thanks to his marketing team's idea to bring the public in on the changes at the House of Lamon, he had agreed to pick a spokesperson for the new shoe line. An ordinary woman with extraordinary style. That was how they'd approached this out-there promotional ploy. He had to assist every one of them with slipping on this new pair of shoes in hopes of finding not only the perfect fit, but also the perfect package. A spokeswoman for the new line of Lamon shoes, purses, and clothing hitting the stores this spring. Someone who bespoke of that elegance and grace Castle's was trying so desperately to hold onto.

But ... why wait? He knew which woman he wanted to wear his latest creation.

Her. The woman in red who was already wearing a pair of Lamons. And wearing them very well.

"I'd like—"

His request was cut off by Caron's loud announcement on the microphone someone had shoved into her hand.

"Thank you all for coming to Castle Department Store's annual Valentine's Gala and our one-hundredth anniversary," she said, her severe gray wool pantsuit making her look like she'd stepped out of a fashion spread. "We always enjoy spending Valentine's Day with our clients for this wonderful fundraising event, and though my dear husband Charles is quite ill and couldn't be with us, we are especially excited to have the infamous and handsome Nico Lamon of the Lamon Fashion House here all the way from Italy. Mr. Lamon and his rather large entourage are here to help us celebrate the last century in a big way."

Everyone clapped. Nico smiled and searched the dazzling overly decorated first floor for the woman in the red dress. Where had she gone?

Caron explained how the event worked. Nico still couldn't believe he'd allowed his marketing team to talk him into doing this. It was a brilliant idea, but why couldn't one of them handle it? If they had, he could have ditched the tuxedo, went out to the Ft. Worth ranch where his mother had been raised, and truly enjoyed himself. Alone. Or maybe with the woman in red.

Nico remembered why he was here. The House of Lamon was making a comeback in a big way. And while he hadn't forgiven his deceased father for having a wandering eye that had ended his parents' marriage, he wanted to keep this company strong. For his mother's sake and to appease his own guilt.

He didn't have time to dally. But ... the woman on the stairs made him wish he did.

When a round of applause brought him out of his dark memories, Caron stared at him, her hand over the mic. "Are you ready?"

"As ready as I'll ever be," Nico replied, his English as natural as his Italian. "But I saw a woman—"

"We have many willing applicants, as you can see," Caron said, her lipstick a little too much on the blue side of red. "If I were younger!" She wagged a painted fingernail in his face. "But ... even though my Annabelle seems disinterested, I think she'd make a great spokesperson for the Lamon shoe line, don't you? I mean, look at her. She's skinny, and her feet are so dainty."

Nico glanced at the lovely Annabelle just in time to see her pop a bubble with her green chewing gum. "She is slender, I'll give her that." He glanced at her feet. Dainty would not be the word he'd choose to describe those feet. They weren't bad. Tiny and ... well ... bony. Doable, but not what he had in mind. He needed a more mature attitude.

"I have to abide by the contract, Mrs. Castle," he said on a gentle note. He watched his entourage line up the giggling, perfume-infused women who looked like wilted flowers from his mother's summer garden. Or a bevy of those bachelorettes from that show his younger sister Cara loved to watch. Cara would fit right in here, but she was off traveling the world.

"Oh, you mean the stipulation about allowing all the young women who bought a ticket to try on the shoes?" Caron asked, her chin drooping.

"Yes, that one." But he'd break the contract if he could find *that* woman. The one with the shimmering gold hair and gorgeous ankles. And the best feet. Somehow, he knew she had good feet.

"Well, consider her when she sits down, will you?" Caron asked on a nasal whine. "The girl needs something to focus on besides Mick."

Having seen the goth-infused Mick, Nico could certainly understand Caron's need to keep Annabelle busy.

"May the best foot win," he said into the mic to get things moving. Maybe this would go quickly, and he could go find the lady in red.

Then he proceeded to offer up his latest creation to every feminine foot that came his way. Before long, his back hurt from bending over and his head throbbed from the many exotic scents in the air, the constant sounds of shrill giggling, and the drawling flirtations.

An hour or so later, he finally glanced up to find Annabelle glaring at him. "Mother insists I try on your stupid shoes."

Nico gave her a cautious glance. "By all means, why don't you?"

He'd just managed to lift Annabelle's black stilettoes off her *dainty* feet when he caught a flash of red chiffon in a departing swish near the entryway to the store. He'd liked her from the front, but he was definitely in love with her departing back.

The dress dipped along her backbone. Still modest and ladylike, but low enough to show her creamy slender neck and alabaster skin. The diamonds winked at him again as she hurried in the other direction.

One last foot and he'd find her, somehow.

When Annabelle let out yelp that startled all the matrons sipping champagne, Nico glanced down. The shoe didn't fit. At all.

"That hurts," Annabelle griped, shoving her red foot toward him. "Get it off, now!"

"Of course." Nico obliged with an immense relief. "I guess you were my last hope."

"Ain't gonna happen," Annabelle said, her purple lips turned down. "No matter that my mother thinks she can make anything happen."

"You do have lovely feet," Nico said, standing and holding the red satin shoe with the sparkling crystal-embossed bow on the toe.

"Right," Annabelle retorted. "What every girl wants to

hear. Do you have a foot fetish?"

Shocked, Nico shook his head. "No, I just enjoy creating beautiful, wearable art for ... elegant, intelligent women."

Annabelle frowned, realization coloring her expression. "Whatever."

Her mother grabbed her arm as she tried to get way. "Where are you going?"

"To find Mick," Annabelle retorted. "This is ridiculous."

"The shoe didn't fit your daughter," Nico said, daring Caron to make a scene.

"I can't believe you didn't find anyone," Caron said on a rush of disappointed breath after her huffy daughter pushed by her. "What do we do now? This is a disaster. Didn't you plant a model in here somewhere—at least to save face?"

Nico wished he'd thought of that idea. "No, I didn't," he replied. "It's a standard size. I don't understand why—"

Then he saw her, coming straight up the aisle, the dress swirling around her like liquid fire, the diamonds almost grinning at him now.

"I think we have one more," he said, smiling at the beauty walking toward them. Maybe she'd decided she'd like to try on the shoes.

Caron glanced around, looked the woman up and down, and gulped in a bewildered breath. "Oh, dear. Where in the world did she come from?"

Chapter Three

WHEN ELEANOR HAD come down the marble staircase earlier, too many memories had assaulted her and a wave of nostalgia crushed her. The sparkling silver and red Valentine's decorations—giant red hearts, fresh-cut fragrant roses in crystal vases, and silver cupids grinning here and there—only reminded her of all she'd missed for the last few years.

She missed her mother tonight, too. Vivian Castle, ten years younger than Eleanor's father, had possessed the kind of style and class that brought Grace Kelly to mind. But her mother had also possessed a beautiful heart. Eleanor could only hope she'd someday fill her mother's shoes. She'd almost ran back upstairs to hide out in the dressing room, her turret room when she was younger, but then she'd seen him.

Nico Lamon.

Now she couldn't stop thinking about earlier when she'd stared directly down into Nico Lamon's eyes. He'd given her a second look, but she knew there was no way he could recognize her. She'd changed since that one chance meeting when she'd been a frightened, heartsick teen. And yet, the air around her had sizzled with a sweet awareness when his gaze had moved over her.

That certain *something* had been there between them. The chemistry she'd felt all those years ago, a tingling down her spine, an awareness weighing at her heart, had resurfaced along with her doubts. She needed to remember that he was good at charming women.

Eleanor decided she'd better stick to her mission. Clearing her head, she scanned the floor again, amazed at the glamorous people vying for Nico's attention. This night seemed frivolous, but the Lamon Fashion House had been around for three generations. From what she'd heard, Nico had reluctantly taken over when his father had died five years ago.

And turned it into a powerhouse that was slowly making a climb back into the retail world. All the more reason for her to be here to protect Castle's. She needed to make sure this deal was done with the upmost caution.

She's stayed on the fringes of the crowd, watching and absorbing, but she finally pushed through and started toward where Caron was standing with Nico, but only to get a better view of the suspicious customer seemingly engrossed in finding the perfect ring at the jewelry counter.

But her gaze kept moving back to *him*. Nico sure knew how to wear a tuxedo. Obviously, the man had a good tailor. Taking another covert glance at him, she actually sighed. His dark hair brushed his collar in rich waves, making him look like a pirate, and his eyes were a midnight blue, bordering on black. His face held shadows and a roughness that only made him appear more dangerous. Eleanor took her time admiring him before she checked on the jewelry department again, noting that the store's current top security man, Johnny Darrow, was also watching that area.

Good. She was about to do another round when she happened to take one more glance at Nico Ramon.

And found him staring right back at her, his gaze holding onto her in an intimate way that left her just a bit breathless. Or maybe that was from hurrying in these high heels.

Gaze still on her, he took the mic from a nearby technician. "I think we have one more woman here tonight who should try on my Valentine shoes."

Everyone craned their necks toward Eleanor. Confused, she glanced behind her, figuring they had a straggler.

Nothing but old rich men in stuffy tuxedoes and their bored wives.

When she turned back, Nico was looking at her with that intimate hope again, his eyes full of a suggestive promise. But Caron seemed to be close to foaming at the mouth. Oh, this was getting good, but she had to hurry away before things got out of hand.

"Stop," Nico said, beckoning to her. "Come and sit on this chair, please."

"Me?" Eleanor shook her head, the soft growl of his slight accent shimmying down her spine in a delicious dance while the firm tone of his command made her want to inform him she did not take orders. Instead, she mumbled, "I ... I can't do that."

"I insist," he said, shoving in front of Caron. "I'd hate to leave without letting the most beautiful woman in the room try on my latest creation." Taking Eleanor's hand, he looked into her eyes. "What's your name?"

"I can't..." Eleanor tried again, panic setting in. He was using his charms on her, but she wouldn't fall for it. She couldn't tell him her name, either. Not her real name and not her nickname. "I need to go."

"What she means," Caron said, stepping around Nico, "is that she can't because she ... wasn't on the guest list, and we don't know who she is." Pointing to Eleanor's empty hands, she added, "She needs a ticket to try on the shoes. I think this woman crashed our gala, and that's why she won't tell us who she is."

"She's correct," Eleanor said. "I mean, I didn't crash, but I left my ticket in the powder room. Besides, I'm not at liberty to be a part of this."

"Really?" Nico asked, grinning again. "Are you a model? Do you have an exclusive contract?"

"You could say that," Eleanor said. She almost wished Caron would toss her out. "I'm ... I'm not a model. It's so nice of you to think of me, but this isn't my thing. Not at all."

"See," Caron said. "She's embarrassed. I mean, I certainly understand how some women would try to worm their way in to try on these exquisite shoes. And meet you, of course. But we don't allow such shenanigans here at Castle's."

Eleanor almost snorted at that self-righteous speech. Instead, she said, "I was invited by one of your employees to be her guest, but I don't have a shoe ticket."

Nico glared at Caron. "Is there something in her demeanor that says she can't try on a shoe?" Leaning close to her stepmother, he said, "Indulge me, please, in the same way I indulged you by letting your adorable daughter Annabelle try on these shoes."

Caron studied his face, apparently seeing what Eleanor saw—a steely determination and a definite power. A dare, too.

Caron stuttered, a first. "Well … we … will look bad if these infuriating shoes don't fit someone. Then this whole stunt will become a PR nightmare. I can't let that happen."

"Exactly," Nico replied, obviously proud of himself. "So you'll agree there is no good reason this lovely lady can't slip on these shoes?"

Eleanor's bones seemed to melt. The man was even better looking up close, and he smelled like a forest in the rain. His eyes were so dark. So, so blue. And that hint of an accent had her enthralled. Not to mention those gorgeous shoes. And he was defending her honor, something that seemed so old-fashioned and romantic she actually felt another sigh coming on.

She almost gave in.

Caron sputtered and tried to find a way to stop this. People were staring, however, so she recovered with practiced aplomb, an angry resolve on her preserved face. Answering Nico's question through clenched teeth, she said, "No, nothing I know of, and I did allow the employees to bring a plus-one."

She moved to Eleanor, her shrewd gaze pinning her to the spot. "Put on the shoes so we can get this fiasco over with, won't you?"

Afraid Caron had figured out her real identity, Eleanor tried to find a way out of this situation. "But..."

"But you will indulge our guests and Mr. Lamon, won't you?" Caron said, her brown eyes turning as dark as coffee grounds. "Do it, or invitation or not, I will have you thrown out."

Eleanor didn't want to make a scene and risk someone recognizing her. Most of these people didn't know her since she'd stayed in the background in the past, but what if someone knew her secret and decided to announce who she really was? With everyone in the place watching her, Eleanor wanted to run and hide like she'd done all those years ago.

Nico's velvet eyes held her. "Don't be nervous. You're already wearing one of our best sellers. These are going to fit beautifully."

He held up one of the red satin pumps lined in silver leather. "This is the kind of shoe that makes a woman feel confident and special."

Special. Just being back here made Eleanor feel special, but it also made her feel dejected and horrible, too. But Caron's glaring gaze and harsh words made Eleanor straighten her spine and remember her true mission. She had to oust this interloper and help her father.

"I'm not nervous. In fact, I'd love to try on your shoes," she finally said with a slight smile. "And then, I really have to go, so if you want to toss me out afterward, *Mrs.* Castle, go ahead."

Caron made face, about to become all bluster.

But before she could form a comeback remark, Nico swept his right hand out and bowed. "At last, I get to meet the woman in red."

Chapter Four

NICO GUIDED THE woman onto the red satin stool, the touch of her soft skin making him wish for moonlight nights and the sea nearby. She had a shyness about her that intrigued him, but there was strength there, too. Now that he had her up close, he could see her true beauty. Her eyes were a light sky-blue, almost like opals or moonstone jewels. She had high cheekbones and a classic oval face with just a few pretty freckles across her pert nose.

Adorable.

There was something familiar about her, but Nico couldn't put his finger on it. A distant memory? Or a soulmate?

His mother, Lila, had always warned him about love. "When you find true love, you'll find your soulmate, someone you'll know instinctively. Or someone you've been waiting for all of your life. That's how it happened with your father and me. I knew immediately he was the one."

Could this be *that* woman for him? His soulmate? Not likely. He didn't need a soulmate. The one he'd been waiting on all of his life? He wasn't waiting for any one woman. All of this Valentine's romance was getting to him. He'd staked so much on this comeback. His company's reputation depended on it. While he'd made great strides in bringing Lamon out of the brink of bankruptcy since his father's death, he knew he still had a long way to go.

But with this beauty, he might just pull it off.

"Are you enjoying the gala?" he asked quietly, the floral scent surrounding her filling his senses like a forbidden garden. He bent to one knee, putting the shoe on the floor in front of her before touching a hand to her arm to make sure she wasn't going to bolt.

She slanted him a stare, her eyes full of confusion and resistance. "I was until ... you grabbed me and brought me over here."

She kept glancing toward the jewelry counter where a sharp-dressed man in an ultra-sleek brown tux moved about. But another man, also well dressed, stood talking to one of the associates who was showing him a chocolate-diamond necklace.

"Is that your boyfriend, the one in the interesting tux? Or maybe the other man? He looks like he has money."

She lifted her head to stare at the men. "No, no. Not at all." Then she frowned at him. "Do I look like I need a man with money?"

"No, of course not." Realizing he'd insulted her, he added, "I'm being nosy. Never mind that."

"I should go," she replied, clearly not impressed with him or the Lamon shoes.

"Not just yet."

Nico removed the silver pumps from her pretty feet. He admired her dazzling red toenails dotted with white hearts and her shapely legs. "But you'd rather be over there. Is there someone else you're searching for?" He kept his tone low, so their conversation stayed private.

"Who? What?" She looked surprised as she tossed another brief glance over her slender shoulder, but she spoke in a hushed voice as well. "No, no. I think one of them works here. And I'm not so sure about the other one. I don't know him." Facing him directly, she said, "I have to be honest, I love chocolate diamonds. I was on my way to the jewelry counter when you stopped me."

"Oh, so I'm distracting you from your real mission?"

Her eyes widened, one hand moving to her necklace. "Mission? I'm not on a mission."

"Relax," he said, grabbing one of the red pumps in one hand as he lifted her foot with the other. "I know I've put you on the spot, or maybe in the spotlight, but … it's going to work out. I had almost given up hope, but now that you're here, I have a good feeling about this."

"I don't have that good feeling," she replied, watching his face as he put the shoe on her right foot with a bit of dramatic flourish. Nico heard the crowd sigh. When she glanced down, she let out a little gasp, her gaze lifting to him in awe. "Oh, what a gorgeous shoe. So elegant."

"One of my favorites," he said. "We worked hard on making these shoes perfect for a romantic Valentine's night. And now that I see this shoe on you, I think it was worth all of this fuss."

"And it fits me," she said, wonder in that admission. "How is that possible?"

"To perfection," he replied, focusing only on her. "It's possible because this shoe was made for this foot. These shoes were made for you and only you."

"I've never heard that line before," she whispered, her lips slightly parted as she gazed at him.

"It's not a line," Nico said, wanting her to believe him. "I only went along with this promo stunt because, in spite of my reputation, I believe in love and romance, and I wanted to find the right woman for this job. I think I have."

She studied him. Really looked into his face as if she'd just now seen him as someone she might enjoy getting to know.

"You do have a reputation," she murmured. "And not in a good way."

"Don't believe everything you see or hear," he replied, trying to hide the irritation he felt because he knew she was right. At one time, his reputation had been bad.

She lifted her chin a notch. "I know all about reputations and how they can be destroyed. I try not to judge too harshly."

Relieved, he smiled. "Then you truly are a classy lady."

They stayed that way, staring at each other for a few heartbeats. Nico thought he might be ill since his heart kept bumping too fast and he felt lightheaded. He'd never felt like this before.

Then Caron cut in, voice tight. "Well, get on with it already."

The woman shot Caron a look that said many things, the first clearly conveying she needed to back off. It only made

Nico like the beauty even more.

But then she tried to stand, one foot bare, the other sheathed in red satin. "Okay, so this was a nice little moment, but I need to—"

"Put on the other shoe," he finished. Urging her back down, he took her left foot so he could slip the shoe over it. After doing so with care and taking his time because her skin was so soft, he said, "Now, why don't you walk around in them? For our patrons and the cameras. And because I want to see you in the shoes."

"Cameras?" she said on a soft croak, that doe-like panic in her beautiful eyes again.

Was she an introvert who'd just now ventured out? A rich recluse who was forced to make an appearance? Or maybe she'd run away from a brutal but rich husband. Nico had to find out who she really was. And he wanted to find out about that trace of hurt he'd seen in her eyes.

"Are the cameras necessary?" she asked.

"Of course." He held out his hand, helping her from the stool when she reluctantly took it. "Because you are about to become the Lamon Lady, the woman who not only knows how to wear a pair of shoes, but who is strong, classic, and determined, who carves her own path and always puts her best foot forward with elegance and grace."

He saw the shock registering on her face, the fear cresting in her expression. "I can't do that—"

"Yes, you can," Caron whispered from behind him, the hissing sounds of her words making him think of vipers. "If the shoe fits, you will wear it for now."

Caron faced the crowd. "Meet the new Lamon Lady."

The crowd went wild. Tiffany from Cosmetics, who'd been so kind to Nico and his team, was clapping, shouting, and waving. Apparently, she approved. And maybe she knew who this beauty truly was.

"You need to tell us your name," Nico said, waiting, hoping.

"But I can't be anyone's spokesperson," the woman said, staring in shock toward the sound of applause—some of it genuine, some of it polite, and some of it downright hostile.

Every woman in this place wanted to be her right now, but they all hated her at this moment, too.

Nico had the sudden urge to pick her up and whisk her out the door.

"Just go with it for the next hour," Caron said, her smile as fake as her eyelashes. "And then, whoever you are, you can leave. We'll come up with a good reason why you can't fulfill the duties of spokesperson. Annabelle will step in, of course."

Nico would not let that happen. "We'll discuss this later, yes. Right now, let's celebrate by dancing." He took the beautiful woman by the waist. "*Vieni, bellezza.*"

"I don't dance," she said. "And I really need to go."

She kept darting glances at the jewelry department. Women. They loved diamonds almost as much as they loved shoes.

"What if I dance you over to the chocolate diamonds?" he offered. Anything to keep her near. "We can look at the jewels together. The crowd should love that."

"Great idea." Caron addressed the eager crowd. "It seems

we have a winner! Let's get this party going."

Everyone laughed and started moving on, but Nico held onto the woman, afraid she'd slip away with all the cameras flashing around them. "What's your name?"

Her eyes became stormy. "Who wants to know?"

"You are charming," he said, his heart doing a private dance. "We need to announce your name. The sooner, the better."

"Do we have to do that?"

"Yes, of course. Monday morning, you'll meet with our publicity people. We'll have to plan out the tour, and you'll need to do interviews. People will want to know who you are, and we'll have to do a background check. Not that I'm worried about that, of course. My team has a whole schedule lined up. Not to mention photo shoots, magazine layouts, and New York Fashion Week."

She pulled away. "I can't do this. I have a job already."

"But we'll pay you twice what you're making. Even more. This is a million-dollar deal."

"What?" She looked so nonplussed and unimpressed he almost laughed. But this was serious business.

They were near the jewelry counter now, and she seemed even more nervous. Was she a jewel thief?

Wouldn't that be ironically delicious? And a PR nightmare.

He didn't even care. "Triple. Three million." He'd have to take out a loan, but it might be worth it.

The woman whirled around. "I can't be your spokesperson, Mr. Lamon. And I can't explain why right now, but—"

A commotion behind them caused her to whirl around.

Then everything went crazy. Alarms started going off, and people started running. "Thief," someone shouted. "Stop him."

The man in the sleek brown tux sprinted after the figure shrouded in a dark mask and black suit that had appeared out of nowhere and grabbed a velvet-lined box of sparkling rings.

"This can't be happening," Caron said on a loud moan. "Where is security?"

Nico glanced around, prepared to protect his Lamon Lady. Instead, he was shocked to see his beautiful spokesperson had also taken off. He saw her running in the same direction as the brown tuxedo man and the masked robber, her dress flowing behind her like liquid silk, her golden hair falling away from her neck.

And she was still wearing the Lamon Valentine shoes.

Chapter Five

ELEANOR DIDN'T STOP to think. All of her senses were on catching the thief. Turned out it hadn't been the man standing at the counter but someone else who was probably his accomplice. So she ran, hurrying to catch up with Johnny and find a way to get those expensive jewels back.

"Have you alerted the security staff?" she called to Johnny as she came to the big landing to the main entry of Castle's.

He looked back briefly, taking the stone steps to the sidewalk two at a time. "Of course. 9-1-1 as well. And … who are you?"

The suspect was turning a corner onto another block, the closed jewel box tucked under his left arm. Eleanor heard a motor revving. Stopping for only an instant, she kicked off the beautiful red satin pumps. Tossing them off to the side of the top step, she ran barefoot past Johnny.

"Hey, who are you?"

Ignoring the question, Eleanor whirled around the side of the building in two seconds. Up ahead, she spotted the man who'd been wearing a black domino mask sprinting toward a waiting vehicle out on the curb.

Eleanor accelerated, her bare feet scraping against the

cold concrete, her hair now in shambles around her face and down her back. With a final push, she rushed the culprit and grabbed him by the collar of his expensive black jacket before shoving him hard, forcing both of them to fall.

Eleanor heard him cry out in pain when he hit the pavement, but she landed on top of him and held him down. Calling over her shoulder, she said, "Hurry."

Sirens echoed in the distance. She had to get out of here before everyone came to find them.

Johnny rushed up, out of breath. "I got him." He held the man down with one strong arm and a booted foot, while he helped her up with his other hand. "Again, who exactly are you?"

"I'm your new boss," she said. "But if you tell anyone about this, I'll fire you. You never saw me, understand?"

Johnny looked shocked, his brain seeming to stall. Then he looked amused, his let's-break-some-rules creed clearly intact.

With a grin, he said, "I won't forget *you*, boss. But hey, I never saw you. Never saw you tackle this lowlife who seems to want to live the high life. And you did it in a red dress and those shoes everyone's talking about. No, I never saw any of that."

"I *saw* her and I'm suing," the man—a very young, scared teen—said. "I think she knocked out my tooth. I'll tell everyone what she did. My dad is a very powerful man. He'll take care of this. I'll tell everybody I know what you did to me."

"And you tried to snatch and run with about a half-million dollars' worth of jewels," Johnny retorted, his nose an inch from the shaking kid's face. "Who do you think they'll believe?"

"I'll explain later," Eleanor promised. Then she glanced at the thief. "Why did you even try?"

The boy shook his head. "Just for kicks. You wouldn't understand."

Johnny hauled the teen up, and shoved him back toward the store's main entryway. "I'll try to understand, cause, buddy, you've got some explaining to do." He stopped and turned back to Eleanor, "Hey, I want a raise."

"You got it," Eleanor said over her shoulder. She had only seconds to get through the back security door and out of this dress.

NICO FOLLOWED SEVERAL other people out the doors, still shocked the woman in red had taken off. Why had she run away? She'd obviously used the commotion of the robbery as a distraction to escape. Had that been part of the plan? She'd distract everyone by playing coy while she tried on the shoes? Just so her partner could steal some chocolate-diamond rings?

Was she in on this heist?

Where did she go?

He hurried onto the steps from the entryway to the street, and looked both ways. People were rushing around, some confused, some screaming. Sirens echoed over the city.

A police car skidded to a stop out on the street.

Nico didn't know which way to go so he whirled to go back inside and search for her there. Something lying on the far corner of the curved steps caught his eye.

A pair of discarded red shoes.

"What is going on around here?" Caron said, pushing at him to get down the steps.

"The thief got away," Nico said. "The police are here. Did you see where she went?"

"Who? I thought a man stole the jewelry."

"The woman in red," Nico replied, annoyance and fatigue coloring his words.

Caron let out an aggravated huff. "No, and right now I don't care. This night has gone from bad to worse."

Nico moved past her, and hurried to the curve in the steps. Bending, he picked up the beautiful shoes he'd only minutes ago placed on the woman's slender feet. "I never even got her name," he said.

His gut told him he probably wasn't supposed to know her name. Now he wanted to know what kind of game she was playing and why.

Another commotion ensued down on the sidewalk.

The brown-suited man came stomping up to the police officers, shoving the shoplifter in front of him.

Caron let out a yelp of delight. She ran to grab the jewel box, but the man who'd captured the thief held it away. "Sorry, Mrs. Castle. Evidence."

Caron Castle didn't take that very well. "Well, see to it that all of those jewels are accounted for. Next time, do your job so it doesn't happen in the first place."

"Yes, ma'am," the man said on a dry note. He and the police escorted the culprit up the steps, probably taking him to security to be questioned before he'd go on to jail.

Nico stopped the security man. "Excuse me, did you see a woman wearing a red dress come by?"

"Hello, sir," the man replied without answering the question. "Johnny Darrow."

"Nico Lamon," Nico said, shaking his hand. "Did you see her?"

"Yeah," Johnny said after a moment of hesitation. "But like Elvis, she left the building while I was chasing down our thief. Sorry, I don't know where she went. Gotta go, man."

She'd left.

Just like that. Without a word, without a thank you. Just walked away from the opportunity of a lifetime.

And him.

If she was in on the theft, her accomplice would probably turn on her and she'd join him at the jailhouse.

Nico didn't want to believe she could have been involved, but it sure looked that way.

"I must be losing my charm," he mumbled, holding the shoes in one hand while he scanned the nearby streets. He wondered if the valet has seen her. The attendant only shook his head when asked.

Tiffany hurried up to him. "Mr. Lamon, your assistant and Mrs. Castle are up in Mrs. Castle's office. They've been looking for you."

Nico zoomed in on the exotic cosmetician. "Do you

know where she went?"

Tiffany's brown eyes went wide. "Who?"

"You have to know. The mysterious woman in red who tried on my shoes, then ran out the door and apparently disappeared."

"Oh, her. Uh … well … you're right. She had to leave. Something came up. Unexpectedly."

"But you know her, right?"

Tiffany looked so uncomfortable Nico felt bad for asking.

"Never mind," he said. "She's gone now. And I thought she was the one."

Tiffany twisted her wedding band against her finger. "You mean, you thought she'd agree to be your spokesperson?"

"That," Nico said, holding the shoes down by his side and sighing. "And … I thought she might be my 'the one'."

Tiffany slapped his arm, giving him a shocked grin. "No, you didn't."

"Yes, I did," he said, frowning at her. He absently rubbed away the sting of her fingers. "Take these and put them away, please," he said. "I'm going upstairs to hear the wrath of Caron."

"Oh, you won't be the only one," Tiffany said, giving him a sympathetic look. "But, Mr. Lamon, I'll see what I can do about finding your mysterious woman, I promise."

Nico believed her. Tiffany seemed like she knew more than she was letting on.

Come to think of it, a lot of people around here gave off that vibe.

Chapter Six

ELEANOR SLID OUT of the red dress. The waistband was torn, and the skirt had a streak of black sidewalk dirt smeared across it. She knew how much the cocktail dress cost since she'd insisted on paying for it, rather than "borrowing" it the way some socialites did.

A substantial chunk of change out of her new salary. And she had apartment rent coming up. Already off to a bad start.

After she'd slipped into her jeans and white sweater, she tugged on her boots and searched for her jacket. Winter in Dallas could go either way during February, so she tried to be prepared. She'd snuck into the building earlier wearing a black beanie and dark sunglasses. She'd have to sneak out the same way.

This night had not gone as planned. Now her right-hand security man had seen her in action. Since she'd already surmised Johnny didn't exactly play by the rules, she prayed he'd keep her secret. Because she wasn't ready to focus on what had happened with the shoes and Nico, Eleanor thought about Johnny and how he'd handled that shoplifter. She'd done her research on the entire security staff and studied everyone at work when she'd come into the store disguised a few days ago.

Johnny Darrow, the second in command in the security department, was handsome, flirty, and more into Nascar than tuxedoes and parties. He was a rebel in every sense of the word. With his curly golden-brown hair and caramel eyes, he looked like a cross between Johnny Depp and James Dean. But he was good at his job and watched this store like a lone wolf on the prowl. And he seemed to love to torment Annabelle, Eleanor's spoiled twenty-six-year-old stepsister.

Annabelle had grown into a beauty, but she hid her exotic looks behind tons of heavy makeup and an all-black wardrobe that made her look more like a waif than a young lady.

Nothing Eleanor could do about that now, but she was glad Johnny Darrow was around to watch out for her stepsister. At least, she hoped that was all he was doing.

Certain he could handle the reports for the police and anyone else who had questions, she was about to leave the private dressing room when the door burst open. Tiffany barreled inside and locked the door.

"Girl, we need to talk."

"I have to get out of here," Eleanor replied. "Too much happened, and I need to process all of it."

But Tiffany grabbed her arm, bangles jingling down her wrist. "Not just yet, Cinderella. You ran out of there so fast your prince is searching for you right now."

"My prince?"

"Nico Lamon," Tiffany said, dragging Eleanor to a lime-green chaise lounge tucked near a big window that opened out to the Dallas skyline. "He found the shoes, and then he asked about you."

"I can't be his spokesperson, Tiffany. You know that."

"Right," Tiffany said. "I get that you came back here because your daddy's sick and Caron is running the place to the ground, but Eleanor, this man said you might be his one."

"His one to make money and promote his products, yeah, but I can't. I have to find a way to get to my father and see if he's okay… I'm going to take back what Caron's trying to steal from us."

"No." Tiffany took both Eleanor's hands by the wrists and gave her a doleful stare. "Listen to me. Nico said he thought you might have been *the one* for him. As in, forget the shoes and the publicity and let me take you to paradise."

Eleanor's heart did a flip. "He said he wanted to take me to paradise?"

Tiffany shook her head. "Not exactly. But I got the interpretation loud and clear."

"You got what you wanted to hear," Eleanor said, getting up. "I have to get out of here. Nico Lamon will find someone else to promote the Lamon shoes. And I'll never see the man again."

"You might," Tiffany said. "He's supposed to be here for the next two weeks, talking to the press, mingling with clients, and establishing a presence. It's part of the deal he made with Caron."

"Oh, he has a presence all right. The man is gorgeous. Those eyes. That accent. All that dark, curly hair." She looked down at the ruined dress before grabbing a big shopping bag and shoving it inside. "And he stood up for me in front of Caron. He's a real gentleman."

"So you do like him?"

Eleanor whirled toward the door. "What? No. And besides, I thought we were done with him after tonight."

"Nope." Tiffany stood, too, her hands on her hips. "I don't know how you're gonna pull it off, but if you don't want him to figure out who you really are, you'd better look a lot different than you did tonight. Because the man is determined to find you, and he's got the time and money to make that happen."

MONDAY MORNING, ELEANOR marched into the employee entrance to the store, wearing a dark black pantsuit and sensible cushioned kitten-heel pumps that she'd already practiced sprinting in. Her feet were still scratched and raw from running barefoot on the cold jagged sidewalks to catch the shoplifter.

Her heart was a bit battered and bruised, too.

All weekend she'd thought about the predicament she had somehow gotten herself into. She'd been undercover trying to observe things at Castle's, but now she'd become the center of attention.

It had been all over the local news. On television and in the paper. *Mysterious woman runs out of Castle Department Store wearing the one-of-a-kind Lamon Valentine shoes.*

Now she'd done all she could to downplay her looks and

be invisible.

But that didn't stop her from thinking about what might have been.

Nico Lamon might be interested in her?

Eleanor remembered having a huge crush on him, but she couldn't imagine Nico feeling the same way. She'd kept up with his career, and often wondered if he remembered that brief moment when she was so young and had stared at him from the big window of her bedroom. She'd thought about nothing else as she unpacked boxes and admired the view of a small park nestled behind the high-rise near Castle's where she'd rented an efficiency apartment. The place was secure and close enough that she could walk to the store if necessary. Maybe one day she could renovate the old penthouse apartment on the top floor of Castle's and live there.

Like a princess in her tower. That's what her daddy used to say when they'd stay in the apartment. Now it was used for storage. She had to make this work. Castle's was all she had left of her mother. And ... she had to rescue her father, somehow. She was already consulting lawyers and getting the proper procedures in order, but in the meantime, she couldn't tell anyone who she really was. Not even Nico. She didn't have time for a fairy-tale romance, and she had to be practical. Nico would get over whatever he thought he'd felt. He'd just become caught up in the moment, same as her. He needed a special kind of woman to help him, and she needed a special kind of man to understand her.

It would never work.

Eleanor didn't have time to daydream about the past or the future. She had to take care of things in the here and now.

Today, she did look different. She had on her black-framed glasses that held just a hint of tint in the frames and she wore very little makeup, mostly rose-tinted moisturizer and matching gloss with a touch of mascara. Her hair was pulled back in a boring ponytail at the nape of her neck, and she wore a black baseball cap that stated *Castle's Security* in bright red letters.

She barely recognized herself, so she felt confident no one who'd seen her all dazzled up on Saturday night would care about her on Monday morning.

After she'd signed in and put away her bag and lunch, Eleanor adjusted the shoulder holster hidden underneath her blazer and headed into the vast security closet where cameras were set up to monitor the entries, exits, and every floor of the tri-level building. Built on one solid block of downtown Dallas, Castle Department Store was to Texas what Macy's was to New York.

Eleanor Castle was finally back.

"Boss lady."

Eleanor found Johnny giving her an approving once-over. "You dress down nicely."

"Do I look the same?" she asked, thinking the man was too cute for words but so not her type. Apparently, her type was tall, dark, and knew how to make women feel special. "I don't want anyone to recognize me."

"You look different," he said, giving her the thumb's-up

sign. "But red does become you." But then he added, "But you might want to put that hair up. Kind of a unique color."

Eleanor lifted off her hat, coiling her ponytail into a bun before placing it back on her head. "Better?"

Johnny nodded. Grabbing a cup emblazed with a Dallas Cowboys football logo, he poured himself a cup of coffee and gave her a cockeyed grin. "So what gives?"

Eleanor decided honesty would be the best policy since she wanted her employees to trust her. "It's a rather delicate situation," she said. "But I need you to be discreet since we'll be working together for a long time, I hope."

He held up a palm. "Discretion is my middle name. Just call me Johnny *Discretio*n Darrow."

Eleanor slid onto a chair. After a quick scan of the electronic surveillance, she checked the offices attached to this room. "I have to stay undercover. That's the first rule. Mr. Lamon seemed to take a liking to me the other night, but I can't become his model or spokesperson or whatever he needs. I came here to work security, and I want to keep it that way."

"I'm down with that," Johnny said, settling in the chair across from her. Dressed in jeans, he wore a dark jacket and white button-up shirt with an abstract tie. He looked younger and more carefree today. "But why are you doing undercover?"

"That's on a need-to-know basis," Eleanor said dramatically. "I'll let you know one day. I need you to keep me out of things with the shoplifter, as we agreed. For now. You ran him down. You saved the day."

"Got it," Johnny said. "Don't mind that one bit. But ... is this about the discrepancy in inventory we've had recently?"

Eleanor hid her surprise. "It could be, yes. I need you to bring me up to speed on that, as well as on the details of our shoplifter the other night."

"I can do that," Johnny said, standing. "Can you tell me who you are, at least?"

"Ellie Sheridan," Eleanor said. Sheridan had been her mother's maiden name. "I worked security in a big retail superstore before I got hired on by Castle's in Atlanta. When I saw this position was open, I applied."

"And snatched it out from under my nose," Johnny admitted. "But hey, no hard feelings. I try not to complain."

"You'd be great as head of security," Eleanor said. "Don't give up." She'd promote him the minute she became the real boss.

"I won't." He shook her hand. "Welcome, Mrs. Sheridan. Well, I don't even know if you're married, single, or divorced."

"Miss," she said. "Single."

"It's good to have you here, Miss Sheridan."

"Thanks." Pushing away the guilt that gnawed at her for having to lie and tell half-truths, she said, "Call me Ellie. Now let's go talk to the team, and you can introduce me to all of them."

Johnny nodded. "Can I ask one more question?"

"Sure."

"What's the deal with you and the Italian? That man's

been walking around here like a lovesick puppy, asking everyone about the woman in red."

Eleanor's heart did that little bump again. "Nothing there. It was just a moment in time."

A moment she'd never forget. But she didn't tell Johnny that.

Chapter Seven

NICO STROLLED AROUND the store, directing his assistants on how to display the clothes, handbags, and shoes from the spring collection. They'd signed an exclusive deal with Castle's since his mother was born and raised in Ft. Worth, so he wanted it to be right. His family's name and legacy were stamped on every garment and accessory, and this collection was themed with hearts in mind. Not in a frilly way, but in a deep rich reds and vivid spring pinks. In a way that was classic black and rich blue. In a way that showed woman that less was more and more could be attained with a little flare.

So why didn't he feel the sense of accomplishment he'd expected? Why wasn't he pumping his fist and celebrating this new merger with one of the oldest retail franchises in the States? A merger he'd doubted at first, since Caron Castle wasn't the most pleasant person to do business with, and because he'd thoroughly vetted the franchise and saw a lot lacking. Castle's had been struggling, same as the House of Lamon. All that aside, his gut instinct had told him to take the deal. And his mother had loved the idea of getting back to her roots after living in Europe for so long.

He wanted this to succeed, in spite of any doubts. But

this morning, everything seemed to be falling flat.

Because he'd met the woman of his dreams, and she'd disappeared. Nico usually didn't obsess about women in this way. His parents had loved each other to distraction, sometimes ignoring both their children and their vast holdings. Until one day, when what seemed to be the perfect marriage had ended and they'd announced their divorce. His American mother had moved to the South of France. And his father had continued at the Lamon Fashion House.

Alone.

They'd lived apart but still loved each other to the very end, which only confused Nico. His mother called the arrangement civilized. Nico called it crazy, and it had sent him way too many mixed messages about love and marriage.

Nico had decided early on that while it was nice, and he admired their loyalty to each other even if it did confuse him, he'd be more footloose and fancy free, taking care to never become distracted by emotions, so he could keep an eye on things at Lamon. And so he could guard his heart, too.

But he'd failed on both counts. He'd neglected the family business, and he'd run away from love too many times. Nico Ramon liked women. Until now, however, he hadn't planned on going beyond that notion. He'd never stopped to think about the future or the perfect woman for him.

Five years ago, his father had died suddenly of a massive heart attack, and Nico's entire world had shifted. He'd returned to Italy and taken over the business, only to find things were not as they seemed. While putting on a brave front, his father had never recovered from the divorce. They'd almost lost the Lamon Fashion House, but Nico had fought and scraped and hired the best of the best to help him create and design classic Lamon products. He had to make this work.

It should be working, but ... he wanted to find her.

A woman who'd stirred his senses. She was the missing piece. And in spite of asking everyone who worked here and going over the invitation list, he couldn't find out anything about her.

No one knew who she was or even how she'd gotten into the gala. Caron screamed at anyone who mentioned either. Anabelle scowled and pretended to be working at the accessory counter, but she mostly posted to several social media accounts and flirted with Johnny Darrow, trying in various ways to embarrass her mother.

And Aidan, the quiet older brother, had made a quick appearance at the gala and then he'd left with the first blonde who'd flirted with him, so he hadn't even seen her.

Nico remembered those days.

The one bright ray in this dust-up—the local media was all over it, plastering pictures and live video from the gala online, on the air, and in the local magazines and papers. So today, the store was full of anxious women wanting to catch a glimpse of the beautiful lady who'd left the Lamon Valentine shoes behind. They also wanted to buy shoes. Any shoes that had the famous black Lamon L elaborately scrolled on the soles.

At least they'd exceeded their projections on that account.

For the tenth time, Nico's assistant Mira Bianchi came hurrying to his side. Mira was a little over four and a half feet tall. She was like a second mother, but she was also a fierce gatekeeper, mentor, and organizer who kept him on task. Today, she had on her round, black-framed glasses and an exquisite navy-blue Lamon sheath paired with gleaming pearls that shouted *understated*.

"Nico, really, we've got to issue another statement to the press," Mira said in her clipped Italian-accented English. "They want to know about the Lamon Lady—you know, the reason we all came here in the first place, *capisci*?"

"I'm working on that, Mira. As I've already told you."

"I understand," Mira said, her silver hair springing out around her forehead and ears like threads of silk. "Work faster. We need to find a spokesperson."

Nico knew she was right. "I'm mulling things over until I have a new plan. Meantime, we'll keep spinning this. That's all we can do." He summoned the team following him around, all young, edgy, and completely up to date on the latest in technology. "Make her mysterious. She had to rush off to Greece or she was late for a rendezvous."

Which is what he kept imagining. Whirling to straighten a pair of heavy denim skinny jeans, he said, "Or better yet, put out a search for her."

"How? We don't even know her name."

"Just call her The Woman in Red or the Lamon Lady. That's who she is."

Deciding that was that, he tried to put the missing woman out of his mind, so he could get down to business. He had to get this collection up and running.

ELEANOR STARED IN the mirror, Tiffany standing behind her wearing Valentine-embossed earrings and a sleek black sheath.

"Are you sure about this?" Tiffany asked, her pert nose scrunching in distaste.

"For now, yes," Eleanor said. She lifted her hands to the wig Tiffany had purchased in the hair salon upstairs. The blunt brown bob was a drastic change from her golden locks. "It does match my glasses."

Tiffany adjusted the back of the wig. "Yep. And makes you look like either Buster Brown or a ninja warrior."

"I can be both," Eleanor said. "Now I have to go and meet the evil queen."

"I hear that," Tiffany replied. "She is close to chopping off heads as we speak. Caron is not happy about the gala's dramatic ending, but she did hold a press conference with your prince a few minutes ago."

"He's not my prince, Tiffany. We discussed this. I only met the man for close to five minutes."

"Right. Okay. Whatever." Tiffany rolled her eyes and checked her lipstick.

"I know about the meeting," Eleanor admitted, hoping to stay off the subject of Nico Lamon. "I sent Johnny to give a security report earlier, but I'll make it to the meeting. I still have to meet with my staff, too. But Johnny and I agreed that a disguise might be better since my hair kept falling out of my cap."

"Johnny's a good man," Tiffany said. "He's got a thing for Annabelle, but she's so clueless. It's really sad."

"Does he want to date her? I mean, she's such a brat."

"I think he'd like that, but Annabelle is all about Annabelle," Tiffany said. "And she loves to mess with her mama's head, of course. Caron wants her to become the Lamon Lady, but that girl would need to learn how to *be* a lady. I think the spoiled-brat appearance is just for show."

"Are Annabelle and Aidan close?" Eleanor asked, worry for her siblings nagging at her brain. They weren't that much younger than her, after all.

"They're close," Tiffany said, "but they travel in different circles. Annabelle is all about becoming the next social media star, but Aidan is more introverted and behind the scenes. He's a whiz at anything technology-wise, so his mama stuck him in electronics."

"Electronics, as a sales associate?"

"Yes. But he can do anything from web designs to cyber security. Caron likes to control both of them."

Eleanor took in that sad information. "I wonder if he could influence his sister," she said. "Or maybe Johnny can talk her out of making a fool out of herself all the time."

"I don't know. They go at each other, but ... Annabelle would deck him if he tried to advise her."

"You're right. Johnny might not be a good influence," Eleanor said. She got up to go to Caron's office.

"Oh, I think that would be the other way around," Tiffany responded. "Annabelle would try to get him fired if he even winked at her."

Eleanor wished she could be a true mentor to her stepsiblings, but she had to keep her identity a secret right now. Maybe in a few weeks, she'd reveal who she truly was and let things fall into place.

"I have to find a way to visit my father at the house," she said. "Once I know he's okay, I can move forward on exposing Caron and … getting Castle's up to par. This job is the perfect cover for snooping around to get answers."

"That's a big challenge," Tiffany said, worry in her eyes.

"One I've been training for since I was eighteen," Eleanor said. "I'll be okay, Tiff. I'm going to be very careful."

"You do know about the Valentine's party, right?" Tiffany asked.

Shocked, Eleanor shook her head. "No. Caron carried on that tradition?"

"Not all the time, but this year being the 100th anniversary and the House of Lamon filling the store with inventory, she decided to go for it."

"And she'll want security there, I'm sure," Eleanor said, already getting an idea in her head. "As head of security, I'll be obligated to go. That will get me inside the house."

"Yes, but upstairs is off limits. She'll probably want you to post a couple of your staff in front of the grand staircase."

"I can post myself. And that means I can sneak upstairs to finally see my father."

"That could be dangerous."

"I told you, I'll be very careful."

"Do that," Tiffany said. "Caron is a force to be reckoned with. That woman fires anyone who looks at her the wrong way."

"I'm well versed in the many moods of Caron Castle," Eleanor retorted. "But I'm not that meek, mousy girl who left for college. I can pull out the ninja card when I need to do so. And ... I still have the Castle card." She gave her friend a quick hug. "I'm off to see the impostor queen."

Tiffany checked the hallway outside the dressing room, which seemed to be turning into Eleanor's hideout. "All clear. Hope the meeting goes the way you want."

Eleanor hoped that, too. She went out through the hidden side door. Taking the stairs since they were rarely used, she knew she'd have less exposure to the employees who used the elevators all day long.

When she reached Caron's office, which covered one corner of the third floor, she alerted the receptionist. "I'm Ellie Sheridan, the new head of security."

"And I'm Nico Lamon," a deep voice said from behind her.

Eleanor pivoted, surprised.

Nico stood there staring at her, confusion etched on his handsome face. "Oh, I'm sorry. I don't think we've met."

Eleanor wanted to tell him they had met once long ago and then again at the gala. But right now, she was having a major identity crisis. Hoping he wouldn't recognize her, she smiled and shook his hand. "Nice to meet you, Mr. Lamon. You've certainly stirred things up around here."

And brought my heart out of solitary confinement.

Nico kept staring before saying, "I believe we're both headed in the same direction." Holding out his hand, he gestured for her to go ahead of him.

Eleanor had no choice but to walk with him into Caron's empty office.

Chapter Eight

HER PERFUME SMELLED familiar, and that sultry southern accent reminded him of someone. The features were similar, too. The oval face with the high cheekbones, the creamy, fresh-faced skin. But the dark hair and glasses did not match Nico's memories of the golden-haired woman he'd met on Saturday night. That floral scent that smelled like his mother's garden made him wonder if he should create a new perfume to go with the one classic Lamon scent that continued to be a bestseller. A lot of women seemed to like smelling like heaven.

"Are you new here?" he asked, curious. Taking in the sensible suit and well-made but comfortable shoes, he figured she was all business. And while she reminded him of the woman he'd met at the gala, she could be someone else completely.

He needed to stop obsessing and pay attention instead of expecting *her* to be in every woman he met.

"I started today," she replied in a clipped, authoritative voice, her eye color hidden behind the dark-tinted glasses. "I'm the new head of security. Ellen Sheridan."

"Ellen? I thought you said Ellie?"

"A nickname."

Nico's confusion grew each day he lingered in Texas. His southern-to-the-hilt mother had warned him that he'd be asked many times over, "Who are your people?"

Should he ask this interesting stranger the same question?

"Security? Is that why you're dressed like James Bond?"

She laughed and shook her head. "I have a job to do, which means I dress the part, Mr. Lamon."

Nico couldn't find a retort to that. "I'm Nico," he said, feeling as if he already knew her. "Call me Nico."

She turned away, her gaze roaming around the big, elaborately decorated office as if she thought it might be bugged or loaded with explosives.

Nico had an image of a woman in red running out the door immediately after a shoplifter had taken a box of expensive jewelry. "Were you here for the gala, then?"

Her gaze snapped back to attention. "Technically, no. I was watching and monitoring. We like to stay out of the spotlight."

"I see."

He was about to ask her if she could pull up footage on the main exit, but the door opened and slammed with a swish of an ill wind and another kind of scent. An overpowering and exotic spicy scent that had Nico wrinkling his nose in distaste.

"Caron," he said as he turned from Ellen with a quick smile. "We have a lot to discuss."

"Yes, we sure do," Caron said, her long-sleeved burgundy dress just a tad too tight. Turning to Ellen, she added, "And so nice of you to grace us with your presence, Miss Sheridan.

Normally, I like to meet new employees before they ever hit the floor."

"Good," Ellie or Ellen or whoever she was said, extending her hand. "I haven't been down on the floors yet today. I wanted to meet my staff and ... you, of course. I'm Ellen, but please call me Ellie."

"What an odd name for a security guard," Caron said by way of hello. "I hope you live up to your credentials, Miss Sheridan. And you may call me Mrs. Castle."

Nico watched, amazed, as the other woman bristled ever so slightly before regaining her cool demeanor.

"I've already found several discrepancies in our security," Ellen said, pausing to stare at Caron. "And our inventory shows some declining numbers that can't be accounted for."

Caron touched a hand to the sprouts of hair coming out of her head in a way that made Nico think of Medusa. "What kind of discrepancies?"

Did he hear panic in her voice? Hmm.

"The system is ancient, of course," Miss E said. "No wonder your last officer left. And it's no surprise why we were almost robbed the night of the gala. You need to seriously update the equipment and the electronics. You also need to hire a top-notch security staff to help Johnny Darrow and the others who are very loyal to Castle's. I've already compiled a list of suggestions and an estimated cost for upgrades."

Pushing at her glasses, she added, "I think the inventory shortage stems from unconfirmed shoplifting. Maybe from the inside, but I can't be sure."

Caron's face turned splotchy. "Well, that's a lot to deal with on a Monday morning, isn't it?"

The other woman didn't back down. "I can handle it."

Nico decided Miss E was amazing.

Caron turned the color of her dress. "Why don't we all sit down? I wanted to talk to you both about that very thing."

She took a seat behind the massive mahogany desk, the white leather chair much too big for Caron's petite body.

Miss E gave Nico another quick smile, but he saw the steel behind that brief bit of civility. She was not amused in the least.

Now he had to wonder what the intriguing security guard was up to. Did she know something he didn't?

Caron steepled her highly lacquered fingernails together on the desk. "The gala served its purpose. We've had an upswing in business. Now with Valentine's Day coming up, things are going smoothly. Of course, the women's shoe department sales are off the charts and the Lamon clothing line is flying off the shelves. So that's the good news."

Relief moved over Nico. "That *is* good news. I've talked with many of our clients, and they seem to love Lamon shoes and women's clothing. Caron, I think the incident that happened the other night will blow over."

Caron glared at him as if he'd turned into a troll. "But you still need a spokesperson. Annabelle…"

"Is not a good fit," Nico replied, already bored with that angle. "I'll find the woman in red. I haven't given up. Meantime, I have my whole marketing team on it. They're putting out tweets and placing what few photos we have of her on all social media sites. We're going with—*Who is the Woman in Red?*—for the tagline."

He grinned, proud of his team. "And then we're asking the question—*Are you mysterious enough to wear Lamon shoes?*—in order to generate even more sales."

Caron's frown turned into a pained grimace. "That is brilliant, actually. However, we still need a spokesperson. A real one. Remember, we're to gather at the Castle Estate on Valentine's night. The Lamon Lady is supposed to be the guest of honor."

Nico remembered all too well. But he hoped to have her by his side by then. "We have just under two weeks before that event."

Caron inclined her head. "Yes, and time is running out." Then she pinned Miss E with a daring glare. "That's where you come in, Miss Sheridan. I want you to find that infuriating woman for us. Go through security tapes and check the footage on the parking garage. View every angle, from the streets to the stairs to the elevators. We need to find her. You and Nico can search together, since he seems so enamored of her. Start with her name."

"The Lamon Lady," Nico supplied, turning to Miss E. "She never gave me her name." Then he leaned in, scrutinizing her. "Or maybe she has a lot of names and aliases."

ELEANOR LEFT THE office in a daze. She'd given herself yet

another name in a moment of panic. How could she ever pull this off? Had Nico figured her out already? She wasn't sure. What she did know was she had to get away from him right now, so she could work up a plan.

Caron didn't have a clue because she never actually looked anyone in the eye. She was too busy being all about Caron. The woman had a lot of nerve, sitting in Eleanor's father's chair like a queen, with pictures of her with celebrities and dignitaries lining the wall of that hideously overdone office.

An office that used to be a haven for Eleanor. All masculine and smelling of pipe tobacco, with books lining the shelves and pictures of family on the credenza behind the desk. A cozy leather couch across the room. A view of Dallas outside the window.

A magical, safe place for her to hide away and do her homework or cry because some stupid boy had hurt her feelings. A place where his little Ellie dreamed big and made exciting plans.

But it wasn't like that anymore. No one except her few allies knew she was that little Ellie.

She had to keep at this for her father's sake. She'd been away for twelve years, but she'd kept tabs on him, even when he didn't respond to her letters or calls. She wanted to prove Caron was up to no good, too. And if that took pretending and trying to ward off her feelings for Nico Lamon, then so be it.

She was heading back to security when a strong, tanned hand reached out and grabbed her arm. "Not so quick, Miss

E. We need to talk."

NICO TUGGED HER into an alcove with a window looking out at Reunion Tower. "Want to tell me who you really are?"

Her eyes darkened but she held his gaze, her pulse jumping against his fingers on her wrist. "I told you, I'm head of security. Do you have a problem?"

"No problems," he said. "Just questions. I've been confused since the gala. A gorgeous woman tried on the Valentine shoes I created and then ran off with them."

She flinched, a quick flash before she gave him a blank look.

"Do you know anything about that?"

Facing the window, she said, "I saw it on one of the videos, but I was more concerned with Johnny catching that thief."

"Right. Let's go with that. Did you give chase while you were observing?"

"No, I wasn't here. Officially."

He moved close, so close he could smell the same perfume he's sniffed on his Lamon Lady. "So when you go undercover, do you go deep undercover?"

Her eyes flared with fire. "It's my job."

She sure knew how to be evasive.

"And that's why you're wearing that ridiculous wig and those fake glasses right now?"

"I don't think that's any of your business."

"I'm making it my business."

"You don't know anything about me or this store, Mr. Lamon. You are a guest here for a few days. I suggest you act like one and respect that we all have jobs to do."

"I get that," he said. The little alcove was too isolated and warm, her scent an explosion of spring. "But while I'm here, I'd like to find the woman who almost stole my shoes."

She opened her mouth, but then closed it and pursed her lips. He was deliberately toying with her, testing her to see if she'd slip up. She seemed to be trying hard not to do that.

Giving him an indignant glare, she said, "I'm sorry about your precious shoes, Mr. Lamon. But she did leave them behind."

"Yes, on the steps. Like Cinderella leaving the ball, don't you think?"

"I don't read fairy tales."

"Ah, but you seem to have pegged the evil queen."

"Doesn't take much to see that."

He drew back and studied her. "So … why don't we work together to find the woman and appease the queen? That way, I can get to know you and possibly figure out what you're really up to."

"I'm up to doing my job," she said, recovering. She stood tall and straightened her jacket. "And I have to get back to it."

"That's fine," he replied as she moved to get away. "But I'll be up later today to go through that footage with you. No pun intended."

"Ha-ha," she retorted. "You have a sense of humor."

Nico's stomach roiled with the sure knowledge that this woman was the Lamon Lady. Hiding in plain sight.

Do you really expect her to fall at your feet and confess?

"I do like a good pun," he replied. "But I'm serious about finding this woman. My company has come a long way. This was supposed to be the crowning moment."

"Another unintended pun?" she quipped. Then she turned and hurried away, her flowery scent leaving him more mystified than ever.

ELEANOR MARCHED BACK into the surveillance room and slammed the door. The cool darkness cloaked her.

"Ouch, that bad, huh?"

She whirled to find Claude sitting in a corner with a bottled Coke in his hand. He really did look like Santa Claus and cupid all in one chubby bundle. His white beard shined even in the dark, and his bald head wasn't far behind. He always wore jeans with red suspenders and a crisp, white shirt.

"Pretty bad, yes."

Getting up, he came by and patted her on the hand. "Good to have you back, princess."

Eleanor bit back the tears she wanted to cry. Her daddy used to call her that at times. "Thanks. But I'm no princess."

Claude chuckled. "No, you're even better. You're smart and strong and you're gonna figure it all out. Got it?"

She smiled. "Got it."

After her friend shut the door, she sat down, kicked off her shoes, and thought about what it would be like to kiss Nico Lamon.

Chapter Nine

"ARE YOU SURE you can pull this off?" Johnny said an hour later after they'd gone over the security footage from the gala.

"Well, I don't have any choice, do I?"

Eleanor had narrowed the tapes down to when the robbery had occurred, since they needed to do that for the police anyway. The shoplifter had turned out to be the son of one of their biggest patrons, a woman who spent a lot of money in Castle's.

"Mrs. Gregory is totally embarrassed," Johnny said. "She's begging us not to press charges."

Eleanor gave that some thought. "We have to set an example. Is this his first offense?"

Johnny shook his head. "No."

"He tried to take about a half-million dollars' worth of jewelry, so it's not like he stole a CD or video game."

"Nope."

She swiveled her chair toward Johnny. "What is it you want to say, Darrow?"

"I still can't believe you're Eleanor Castle."

She'd spilled it out to him when he'd came into the security booth earlier, her anxieties overcoming her need to remain anonymous. "I told you we would not speak of that again. I'm Ellie Sheridan until further notice."

"I'm not speaking of it," he said with a wry grin. "But I'm sure thinking about it." He leaned over, his voice a whisper. "I've walked by that mural in the shoe department, like, a thousand times and seen the little girl holding her parents' hands. A little blonde-haired girl with blue eyes."

"Me," Eleanor said, memories of that time piercing her heart. She hadn't had a chance to look at the mural that had been painted by a local artist over twenty years ago. It was too painful, so she'd tried to ignore it. "It was like a dream."

"But you're not ready to tell me the rest."

"Not just yet. Right now, I have to get this footage ready for Mr. Lamon. And if you so much as hint that I'm the woman who's wearing that red dress—"

"I know," Johnny said. "Off with my head."

"I can't thank you enough," she said. "You really are good at your job."

"I'm not going to blackmail you into giving me a promotion," Johnny said, deadpanning. "I want to earn that, but yes, you owe me, big time."

"I do," Eleanor said. "And since you used to be a police officer, you know that sometimes things aren't always as they seem. One day, you'll understand. I hope you'll still be on my side when you do."

He squinted at her in a way that had to melt hearts left and right. "I gave up the streets for something more civilized because I lost someone I cared about. I couldn't deal with death, drugs, and destruction anymore. Burned out, wiped out, tapped out. I have a feeling your story is kind of like that, but in reverse."

"It did start long ago."

"Okay." Johnny stood, squeezing her shoulder once before stepping back to look at her. "I'll guard your secret. It's no skin off my back to know someone might pull one over on Caron Castle."

"What does that mean?" Eleanor asked, wanting information.

Wariness filled Johnny's dark eyes. "I'm not so sure I should explain that to you."

"If Caron has done something you don't like, I want to know," Eleanor said, hoping to win Johnny over.

A knock at the door caused her to jump like a skittish cat. "We'll finish this conversation later. I have to get this together." She straightened her jacket and checked her wig.

Relief colored Johnny's face as he opened the door. "Mr. Lamon, right on time."

Nico walked in and looked into her eyes, his big body filling the tight space with a distinct presence.

"Time for my break," Johnny announced, giving Eleanor an encouraging smile. "Let me know what you decide about the Gregory kid."

"Thank you, I will," she replied, nervous she'd be left in the small surveillance area with the dark prince.

After he shut the door, she motioned to the other chair in front of the monitors. "Please, Mr. Lamon, have a seat."

"Nico," he said, waiting until she sat, his gaze making her feel too warm.

"And you can call me—"

"Ellie," he replied. "If you don't mind."

Eleanor chafed under that steady midnight gaze. "That's fine by me."

He sat forward in the chair. "Show me what you have, Ellie. I really want to find this woman. Not only did the Valentine shoes fit her perfectly, but she fit the image in my head perfectly, too."

"You had a certain image for your spokesperson?" she asked, unable to stop herself.

He nodded. "That and … I have always had a certain image for the woman I might spend the rest of my life with. The golden-haired woman who ran off wearing my shoes fit that image. Completely. Her manners, her style, her regal demeanor." He folded his fingers together and air kissed them. "Perfection."

He'd said all of that in a calm voice that dripped with that gelato-smooth accent while he'd kept his gaze on her the whole time.

Eleanor shielded herself against melting into a pool of mush, trying to find her next thought. "Well, that is indeed a tall order. I didn't think any woman could be perfect. Let's see what we can find."

"Yes, let's do that," he responded. "Because I have a feeling she's closer than we realize."

She had heard of Catch-22 situations but this one was like being caught in a vice. A vice of her own making. She could tell Nico the truth and hope he'd play along, but she wasn't sure how loyal he was to Caron. She knew Lamon's needed Castle's as much as Castle's needed the famous fashion house.

She also knew she was highly attracted to a man she could never have, while he seemed to know everything he needed to about her, maybe even that she was playing a dangerous game. Would he be a friend or a foe?

She couldn't decide right now, and she really couldn't breathe very much either. He was so close. It only reminded her of how he'd stared into her eyes, his hand warm and gentle on her ankle, and put those gorgeous shoes on her feet. He was looking at her now, a deep intensity etching his features. Would he call her out? Since she couldn't be sure, she'd have to keep her secret close to her heart until she could trust Nico more.

He leaned in, just a whisper away. "Show me, Ellie."

"Here we go," she said, clearing her throat. Where did she put that bottle of water? "I pulled up the footage from the gala and found what you requested." She brought the tape up on the screen. "What exactly are you hoping to find? The woman disappeared before Johnny went after the thief."

"I wonder if she was involved in the jewelry heist," Nico replied. "She had an element of mystery about her, so spy-like and criminally beautiful. But I'd hate to see her go to jail for grand larceny."

Criminally beautiful? Eleanor scoffed at that, praying he wouldn't go down that road. But she did run out of the store at the same time of the theft with only a couple of people to vouch for her.

Trying to keep things light, she said, "You are a romantic, Nico."

"Ah, you've discovered one of my secrets. But then, I think we should all be a little romantic. Aren't you?"

"Nope. Not a romantic bone in my body." Sweat formed like webs of lace on Eleanor's backbone. "Do you have a lot of secrets?"

His eyes did a tango over her face. "Don't we all?"

NICO COULDN'T STOP looking at the woman next to him. The dark wig and big glasses were obviously fake. The business suit was quality and the sensible shoes were well-made and sturdy, but the way this woman carried herself only reminded him of the woman who'd run away from him.

Could this be her? Had the woman in red really been Miss E?

Undercover Ellen, security guard, trying to stay undercover? Also known as Ellie?

Maybe Ellie had to stay undercover for security purposes and that was why she wasn't admitting anything to him. She obviously couldn't divulge her tactics, but the least she could do was acknowledge him and explain why she didn't fit his image of the perfect woman.

That had to be why she didn't want the offer he'd made to her, if she was indeed *his* Ellie. Maybe she wanted this job instead of being in the limelight. Which meant she might have a few secrets of her own or that she wasn't cut out to be the center of attention. The last thing Lamon House needed was a disgruntled non-romantic spokesperson.

"Where did you grow up?" he asked, deciding if this Ellie was his mysterious woman, he could play along while he tried to charm her into confessing.

"What does that have to do with you finding your mysterious woman?"

"Just curious," he said, wishing she'd open up to him. "Show me the footage."

She hit buttons and pointed to a monitor. Nico watched, memories of that night clear in his mind. The woman had been hesitant and unsure from the beginning, but after he'd sat her down and put the shoes on her feet, something had happened between them. She'd looked at him with a sweet, awestruck expression and that beautiful gleam in her eyes, as if no one had ever told her she was special before. Or maybe someone had told her that, and she'd just forgotten it.

"Can you rewind and freeze that shot?" he asked, his finger touching the woman on the screen.

She gave him a concerned glance. "Sure, but why?"

Nico leaned close, noticing she'd become fidgety when he moved toward her. This room was small and full of screens and beeping machines. Good thing, since his heart was beating too fast.

"I like that shot," he said, taking his time to explain. "See how she's laughing up at me, surprised the shoes are made for her and only her? For that one instant, we were the only two people in the world."

She let out an unladylike snort, fidgeting even more.

"No, I ... uh ... I don't see that. What I see is a man so determined to find a foot to shove a shoe on, he obviously picked a woman who has no interest whatsoever in them."

Nico touched the screen again before turning to her. "How can you miss it? The way we're looking into each other's eyes, the way her hand touches mine after I place the shoe on her foot. This woman definitely had an interest in *these* shoes. And maybe me. Or so I thought."

Ellie got up, shooting him a look that hovered between a question mark and a deep longing. "What does that have to do with finding her if she doesn't want to be found?"

"Everything," he said, standing beside her. "She left because she's hiding something. I don't think she's involved in the theft, but I do believe she used it as a distraction to get away from the glare of the cameras and the curiosity of the crowd. What could she possibly be hiding?"

"How would I know? We arrested the thief and his accomplice, who was driving the getaway car. And in spite of his wealthy family's need to keep this quiet, we have to press charges."

"I'm not concerned about the thief," Nico said, an acute need to comfort her making him wonder what was wrong with him. "My focus is on the woman I found and then lost."

"Why can't you pick someone else?" she asked, tilting her head. "There were a lot of women at the gala. Surely one of them can make it work with the model-spokesperson-star thing."

Nico pushed further. "What would you know about

that? I mean, fashion, shoes, and ... the need for the perfect face to sell a worldwide brand? Obviously, you deal in keeping this place secure, but I deal with what brings people here in the first place. We seem to be from two different worlds."

She backed away, clearly embarrassed... and hurt. "You're right. I don't know anything about that. Frankly, I don't have time to indulge your need to sit and stare at footage that won't bring the woman back to you."

"I understand," he said, wondering why he'd even said that to her. But it did get a rise. One he wished he hadn't had to witness. "I've seen enough to know what I need to do."

He turned to leave, but turned back around. "If it's not too much trouble, can you show me the footage leading up to where the woman tossed the one-of-kind shoes on the steps?"

"Here," she said, her fingers jamming against keyboards.

Nico stood and watched as the woman raced out the door and down the steps, her golden hair flowing out of its confinements, her dress billowing around her like a blooming rose. Then she looked to the left, tossed off the shoes, and took off running that way.

"Hmm. Interesting that she went off in the same direction as the jewel thief, don't you think?"

"As you so kindly pointed out, what would I know about that? I was observing everyone that night, and I saw a lot of women removing their painfully tight and too-high heels the minute they went out the door."

"Touché."

"Are we done here, Nico?"

"For now," he said. "Ellie."

Then he did leave, with a smile on his face. He'd upset her, but he knew now. This Ellie and his Ellie had to be the same person. But he couldn't let her know that. No, since he only had a couple weeks here, Nico decided he could do a little undercover work himself. He'd find out who Ellie really was, and then he'd produce evidence to prove she might be the woman in red.

And then what?

He'd expose her and embarrass her even more?

Or kidnap her and take her far away?

Or maybe get to know her better and find out why she was trying so hard to keep her identity a secret?

"Smooth move," he mumbled as he left the security office and headed back downstairs to the shoe department.

He'd have to do something to make up for that no-so-nice comment. Something a tough female head of security might appreciate. Then a solution came into his head. A perfect solution to him getting what he wanted—his spokesperson—while also keeping her identity a secret.

Chapter Ten

NICO ASKED AROUND. Did anyone know much about Ellen Sheridan, the new head of security?

Claude, who didn't seem to have a last name, but knew everyone else's, just chuckled and said, "We all keep to ourselves. And she's kind of new. Skittish sort."

Nico didn't need anyone to point that out. "But I need to know more since security is important. You understand."

"You need to talk to Caron about that," Tiffany, the cosmetic whiz, told him when he approached her. "She's not into people asking about her staff. Kind of possessive that way."

"I'll clear things with her and make her see my point," Nico replied.

Claude shot him a shrewd stare. "Be careful. Mrs. Castle has ways of getting what she wants."

Nico tried another tactic.

Standing behind the gleaming counter surrounded by perfumes and creams, the statuesque Tiffany with the exquisite black braids, grinned. "You really want to help Ellie?"

"Yes, I do. I want to show her my appreciation."

"Then just let her do her job." Tiffany motioned him

forward with a lacquered purple nail. "And be kind to her. She's been through a lot."

"Can you define 'been through a lot'?"

"No, I cannot."

Someone was protecting someone around here.

Three days after the gala, he was discouraged, and still working with his team to hold off the press and the crowds clamoring for a glimpse of the new face of Lamon. He liked that the campaign his team had going was at least keeping people actively involved in the launch of the Lamon spring collection.

Social media outlets had gone wild with this. Photos, texts, tweets, and postings were showing up all over the world. Most of them were selfies of women who claimed to be the woman in red, but Nico wasn't buying that. Whenever anyone on his team tried to shove someone else off on him, he shook his head and said, "No."

"And what will you do when we have to return to Italy?" Mira asked this morning while they strolled to the shoe department that covered almost the entire bottom floor of the department store. "We have no spokesperson. We have no plan."

"I *plan* to find her," Nico said while he looked around for a glimpse of Security Ellie.

Mira had his schedule loaded with meetings, television interviews, cooking shows, private dinners, and photo ops that included horses and barbeques. And lots of Dallas debs.

Nico needed some time to think. This campaign was going great, but other than when he was heading up a design team and had a deadline, he liked a quieter, slower pace of life.

"Nico?"

Waving a hand behind him in dismissal, he said, "Mira, I have this under control. Now go and pester someone else."

Mira stood staring after him, her Italian comments flying out in colorful words that made his ears burn.

Nico studied the Lamon Valentine display, all red and white and silver. Decadent and daring. Shoes and sandals and lightweight summer boots of all colors. Like candy waiting to be picked out of a box. The Valentine shoes were front and center, sitting on silver satin inside a locked Plexiglas box since they'd almost gotten lost once before.

He looked up from the display and saw her.

Security Ellie. Nico looked forward to finding her each day, since she became a new woman with every disguise. Yesterday, a blonde pixie wig and teal glasses that matched the teal wool sheath she'd worn with flora embroidered kitten heels.

She stood with her back to him, but he could always recognize her. He knew her from the way she stood. Today, she wore a fitted tan suit and probably a concealed weapon, too. A matching blazer and flared pants in a heavy gabardine hung beautifully over her healthy, athletic body. And a different wig. Short red hair, this time, but he knew her. Period. Her shoes with this prim attire were a bit bold, which gave him hope that she was dropping little hints.

A red-and-gold checkered pattern. Kitten heels, but still alluring. After all, it wasn't the height of the heel. It was the way the woman wore the shoes.

He started toward her, but stopped when he saw she was staring at the mural that covered a big wall centered at the end of the department.

Nico had glanced at the mural, disinterested. But now he studied it to see what interested her about it.

It was a man in a suit with a woman in an elegant tea-length gown and black pumps, walking across a park. In between them was a lovely little girl who looked to be around nine or so, her golden curls hanging down to her waist. She wore a blue dress with a full skirt and cute white shoes with lacy socks.

Her head was turned slightly away as she looked up at her father with a loving smile, and her parents laughed as they stared down at her.

They held her hands on each side, a beautiful Victorian-style dark brick building off in the distance.

Castle Department Store.

Tiffany came by, her head down since she seemed to be avoiding him lately.

"Hi," he said, tugging her to his side. Today, she wore a brilliant blue wrap dress and had her braids twisted around her head like a turban. "Love your outfit."

"Thank you, but what do you want?" Her gaze moved from him to Security Ellie.

"I want to know who is in that beautiful mural," Nico said.

"Oh." She relaxed and gave him her engaging grin. "That is Mr. and Mrs. Castle, about twenty or so years ago. They commissioned a local artist to paint that. Had a celebration to unveil it and a big sale in housewares."

"And who is the child?"

Bubbly Tiffany became sealed-lips Tiffany. "I don't recall?"

"You said that in the form of a question," Nico noted. "I think you *do* recall."

Tiffany gave him a defiant glare, then put her hand on her hip. "Well, if I did recall, it's not my place to talk about such things."

"It's just a mural."

"Oh, that's more than a mural," Tiffany blasted. "It's ... a priceless part of this historic place. A throw-back to another time." She glanced at her watch. "And speaking of time—"

Nico glanced back at the mural, observing the way Security Ellie held her eyes on it. "Wait. Did Mr. Castle have another child?"

"Only one child." Realizing she'd been bested, Tiffany slapped a hand across her mouth. "I gotta go."

Nico glanced between the mural and Security Ellie. He knew Caron had two children whom she'd brought with her into the Castle home. The long-suffering, spoiled Annabelle and the hip, but quiet, Aidan.

Stepchildren who'd been adopted by Mr. Castle.

Did that mean somewhere, a blonde-haired woman close to thirty was walking around?

Or possibly, last seen running away in a red dress?

Eleanor's phone buzzed.

MEET ME IN THE DRESSING ROOM. STAT!

Tiffany?

Eleanor turned from the mural that now brought tears to her eyes. Seeing it up close again made her remember happy times when her world had been colored with balloons, fairy tales, and a security she'd been searching for since.

Today was the first time she'd come down to the shoe department for any length of time. Visiting her favorite department was an indulgence now that she'd settled into her position at Castle's. She shouldn't be here—had asked Johnny and others to do the hourly floor check up until now. But Eleanor had always loved shoes. What woman didn't? After she'd left Dallas and gone off to college, she'd stopped buying and wearing pretty shoes. Too painful, but not in a physical way. Too many softly aching memories and echoing images of better times.

Reinventing herself, she'd become functional and plain. Or even more plain since she'd become that way after Caron came into their lives. Eleanor had been depressed, distressed, and unable to hold onto the confidence her parents had given her, so she'd gained weight, given up on pretty hair and makeup, and didn't bother with stylish clothes anymore. Cupcakes and pizza could do that to a woman.

But after some therapy sessions suggested by one of her college friends, Eleanor had matured and found her own way. And she'd also conjured enough memories to know her mother had instilled a sense of style into her at an early age.

When she'd started going out on interviews, she'd also started shoe shopping again. Now she had quite a collection, a closet full of lovely, timeless footwear that she'd rarely worn.

Until now.

Coming to the shoe department had been a mistake. The mural was still beautiful. She remembered the day the artist who'd been commissioned to paint it had followed them around with a camera to capture the perfect image to put on the wall inside the newly renovated shoe department.

It hurt to think of what she'd lost.

But now, her heart hurt, too. Because she *had* felt something the other night at the gala, when Nico had knelt to place that exquisite red shoe on her foot.

And it had fit to perfection. Both the shoe and the *something*. From the moment she'd come down the stairs and seen him staring at her, Eleanor had felt a surge of awareness that flowed like a cleansing river throughout her system and brought that missing confidence back full circle.

In that moment, she'd looked into Nico's eyes and viewed a reflection of her soul. But she couldn't acknowledge that. The man could ruin everything for her. He was in her way, a beautiful distraction, a throwback to one of those fairy tales her mother used to tell her.

But her mother had always said, "You are a princess, but you have to be more than a pretty face, Eleanor. You have to become a strong, confident woman to make it in this world. Don't wait for a hero to come. Be your own hero."

I'm trying.

Eleanor pivoted to go find Tiffany, her mother's wise words still whispering in her ears. Her mother had been right. She had to be her own advocate. No one else would fight for her.

Not even him. Her prince. The prince she could never have.

She stepped onto the escalator, looking back to see Nico standing in the middle of the shoe department, his questioning gaze following her.

Eleanor's heart wanted her to turn around and tell him her story. But she kept going, her shoes clicking on the tile floor as she hurried to find out why Tiffany needed to speak to her.

Tiffany waited with a wide-eyed expression, tugging Eleanor into the dressing room with a yank of her arm.

"What is wrong with you?" Eleanor asked, rubbing her arm through her jacket sleeve. "Is there a fire?"

"You could say that," Tiffany replied, breathless. "I have five minutes left on my break so I'm gonna speak fast."

"Okay, go."

"Nico is asking about you. He's been badgering me and several other people all week now."

A rush of heat hit Eleanor and sizzled throughout her body. "Why would he do that?"

"Oh, I think that's pretty obvious," Tiffany said, her cobalt earrings dangling like wind chimes. "The man is smitten. I mean, flat out got-it-bad smitten."

"But not with me. With the woman in red."

"I think he's merging the two in his head," Tiffany replied. "And ... he asked about the little girl in the mural, but I played it cool."

"How did you play it cool, exactly?" Eleanor asked, thinking her friend was not that great at hiding the truth.

"I didn't tell him who she was," Tiffany said, shaking her head. "Told him that wasn't up to me to talk."

"You made it sound even more suspicious. Do you think he'll come to *me* about this?"

"No," Tiffany said, checking her diamond-encrusted watch. "But he might go to Caron or her kids. Or Claude again."

"He's been questioning Claude?"

"And anyone who'll listen. Nico has to attend a dinner tonight at some fancy estate but ... he'll be back. He's determined to find that woman—you—before he leaves Texas."

"Well, Texas is a big state," Eleanor pointed out, her backbone misty with perspiration. "He has to leave after the Valentine's party at the estate."

"But the party isn't until next week," Tiffany reminded her. "And Queen Caron wants the entire staff decked out and there."

Eleanor let out a groan. "I know. Security will be in full force. Caron has instructed us to stay out of the way and behind the scenes. I have to sneak upstairs to see my own father while I'm undercover. I wish I could let him know I'm here, but it's too risky right now. I've driven by the house a couple of times, but it's gated with a fancy new security system. I could crack it, but it's too dangerous. Right now, I'm consulting lawyers and gathering evidence."

Tiffany put her hands on Eleanor's arms. "Honey, your daddy is sick. He barely recognizes anyone these days. It sure would do him good to hear your voice again."

"That's why I'm here," Eleanor said. "I stayed away because I was hurt and confused, and his new wife told him lies about me. But I have to get him the help he needs. Find out if he's really that sick or if she's drugging him. I don't care about the money, but I do want the store. I want my father back more than anything. *This* is my home."

"Well then, you'd better do something about that hunky Italian who's roaming around like a bull in a china shop," Tiffany suggested. Then she gave Eleanor a quick hug. "I gotta go."

"Thank you," Eleanor said.

Tiffany grinned and left.

Eleanor turned around to stare out the bay window of this little round room that had always reminded her of a turret.

Right now, she felt like a princess trapped in that turret.

And she didn't see how she'd ever be able to tell her prince the truth.

Chapter Eleven

BOREDOM OVERCAME NICO, but he had to be at this event tonight. Stifling a yawn, he wandered through the huge high-rise apartment in a swanky part of the city, his mind on the mural he'd studied closely this afternoon after Security Ellie had hurried away. Something was niggling at his brain, some distant memory that refused to show itself.

One child. The Castles had only one child, according to Tiffany. Why had no one ever mentioned her? Had something tragic happened? Then he thought about a long-forgotten memory. He'd come here with his parents once as a teenager. Had Ellie been around then? He couldn't stop this feeling of knowing her.

I would have remembered Ellie, he thought. *No way I'd forget that woman.*

He thought about the beautiful mural, and about the woman who'd stood studying it. A woman dressed in an impeccably beautiful and professional suit who wore a red-haired pixy wig. Security Ellie took her job very seriously.

He intended to observe her while she watched everyone else.

Annabelle, who'd been trapped into attending this little soiree with Caron and Nico, sauntered over to where he stood alone near a massive fireplace. Caron had paraded him through the crowd. He'd shared appetizers and drinks with numerous pillars of the community, and promised the rich clients who shopped at Castle Department Store the Lamon Lady would be revealed soon. He'd also told Caron in polite but deliberate terms that no, he did not think Annabelle would become the Lamon Lady, but he was sure she'd find a good future in theatre or being a professional celebrity selfie person.

Caron had not taken that notion very well, but she'd nodded and trotted off in her eight-hundred-dollar brown boots to badger someone else. The woman was both annoying and determined, like a tenacious bulldog that wouldn't let go of anything without a fight.

Now here the waif Annabelle stood, staring at him with doleful black-rimmed eyes. Nico wanted to get out of Dallas and soon, maybe spend a few days at the Double L ranch his mother still owned. But he couldn't leave until he figured things out around here.

"Wanna go out on the terrace?" Annabelle asked. "We can both jump together."

Nico took in the young woman's attire. A black mini-dress that flared out from a tight corset in tuffs of lace with long sleeves. Over-the-knee red patent leather boots and dark hair caught up in pearls and silver.

"You don't want to jump off the terrace."

"Yes, I do."

"Stop that and go have fun."

"I'd rather pull out my hair." To demonstrate, she held

her hands against her cascading curls and tugged harshly.

Annabelle twirled a strand of now-distressed hair around her finger, silver rings catching at it. "I'm bored."

"Me, too," Nico admitted. "Do you attend these type of functions a lot?"

"Nope. The queen wants me to flirt with you."

"You call your mother the queen?"

"She thinks she's a queen."

Glancing across the room where Caron stood whispering into a distinguished-looking man's ear, he asked Annabelle, "Do you like working for your mother?"

Annabelle gave him an elaborate eye-roll. "What do you think?"

Nico smiled. "I think underneath all that kohl and lipstick, you are a beautiful young woman who needs to break free and grow up."

Instead of slapping him, Annabelle actually smiled, her dimples deepening. "That's refreshing. Wow, you design clothes and shoes *and* you're a therapist, too? Go ahead and tell me I'm wasting my life and I need to find purpose."

"I've been there and done that," he replied. "Are you happy, being a Castle? Or do you indeed need to find purpose?"

"I'm not really a Castle," she retorted, petulance in that admission. "Aidan and I started out as Smiths, if you can believe that."

"Rather ordinary, is it not?"

"Yes, but it's my daddy's last name so I like it." Her dark eyes turned misty. "We were happy. We had a little house by a creek, and our daddy was ... like this larger-than-life person. A real cowboy. Taught us how to ride horses and shoot straight, but the queen mother didn't like that. He grew up in Montana, you know."

"I did not know," Nico admitted. "My mother has ties there, too."

"Daddy moved to Texas when he was a teenager. But he always wanted to go back to Montana." Annabelle shot her mother a glare. "But someone didn't want that... so someone cheated on him and made him miserable and ... now I act up as much as possible. Aidan doesn't really talk to anyone, but all the nice girls fall all over him even though he pretends to be a geek. Therapy session over."

Nico decided he could tolerate Annabelle a little better. She needed someone to listen to her, at least. "What happened to your father?"

"He left her, and went all home-on-the-range back to Montana. She drove him to drink, but when he left, he also left Aidan and me." Annabelle shrugged, and lace shimmied all around her like a mourning veil. "She has a way of getting her way, know what I mean?"

"I'm sorry," Nico said, sincere in his heartfelt understanding. "But she remarried, obviously."

"Oh, yes, she dropped the man she'd cheated with when a bigger fish came along. She married *up*. Way up. And she never lets us forget that. Wants us to act like Castles. We actually had to take lessons on just about everything from sneezing to socializing. Made him adopt us after our daddy died." She stared down at the marble floor. "He died from drinking, but I think he really died of a broken heart."

Nico pushed on, hoping Annabelle might give him some insight. "Do you consider Mr. Castle your father?"

"He's a good man, and he tried to love us," Annabelle admitted, her bangles slipping like a slinky down the lace of her sleeve. "But ... he's old and sick." Shrugging, she added, "I had a father. And he's gone now. Mr. C tried to fill in the blanks, but doesn't recognize us anymore. He gets agitated and keeps calling for Eleanor."

Nico's head came up. "Eleanor? Who is that?"

"His real daughter," Annabelle said, glancing around, still bored but definitely ready to talk. "She Who Will Not Be Named."

"Bad blood?" he asked, suddenly glad he was getting to know Annabelle better. The girl was a wealth of inside information.

"My mother hated Eleanor. Eleanor was the real princess of this castle, know what I mean?"

"I'm beginning to, yes."

"She was a few years older than us. First, she tried to like us, wanted to mother us and tell us what to do and not do. But Mother told Aidan and me to ignore Eleanor. Mother also told us horrible things that scared us so we'd pick on Eleanor."

"How old was she then? Not your mother, but Eleanor?"

"A teenager. She was pretty and sweet, but then she got depressed, I guess. I think she missed her mother and ... Mr. C kind of ignored her after the queen had his ear. She became frumpy, didn't dress properly. Gained some weight.

Mother thought Eleanor was trying to get attention. She'd tell Eleanor's father anything to make him angry at his daughter. Then they'd all fight." She lowered her head. "Aidan and I would hide out in the stables a lot."

Nico's pulse quickened with both anger and empathy. For Annabelle and her brother, but mostly for Eleanor Castle. "What happened to Eleanor?"

Annabelle shrugged, and then swung around to face the people moving through the ultra-modern penthouse before answering. "She left for college and … never came back."

NICO COULDN'T SLEEP. So he poured himself a glass of mineral water and opened his laptop to do his own internet search.

But the only thing he found on Eleanor Castle was an old article in the *Dallas Morning News*. Written in 1998, it featured the story about the mural he'd studied today and how it had been commissioned to celebrate Castle's eightieth anniversary and Eleanor's twelfth birthday. A brief history of the store—it had been established in 1918—and the historical aspects of the Victorian-style building that covered one whole square fascinated him. But what fascinated him even more was the caption underneath the photo of the mural.

"Twelve-year-old Eleanor Castle, the apple of her daddy's eye, tells us that, one day, she will be in charge of Castle Department Store."

The article went on with quotes from her parents and

more photos of the loving couple and their only daughter.

"She plans to learn everything there is about retail," her proud mother Vivian explained. "Then she wants to go to college and get a degree in business, so she can follow in her father's footsteps the way he followed in his father and grandfather's footsteps."

Young Eleanor commented, "It's like a real castle, and I get to be a princess. And one day, I'll be the first girl to run the whole chain of stores. But this one is my favorite."

"She already has the run of the place," Charles Castle said. "But her favorite room is the turret room, a private dressing area on the top floor where only the sample models and her mother are allowed to test out women's clothing and shoes. Eleanor, however, uses it as her playhouse."

The article went on to say there was also a private apartment on that floor the Castle's sometimes stayed in during the week. Their grand estate was located twenty miles outside the city.

Nico finished the article, and then he studied the photo of the young girl smiling up at her parents. In this photo, Eleanor's face was close, giving him a good display of her features.

Her father had married Vivian, who was much younger than him, when he was in his late thirties. They'd had Eleanor when he was forty-four. An only child of an older father.

That would now place Charles Castle in his mid-seventies, and Eleanor had to be around thirty-two.

No wonder the man doted on her and his beautiful

young wife. A wife who'd died of cancer three years after the mural had been painted. That had to have been heartbreaking for both father and daughter.

And yet, her father had remarried rather quickly. Caron Smith, who, from what Nico had heard, had worked at a drugstore down the street, had come into his life not long after that.

Eleanor's father had hastily married because of his broken heart. Caron had married up because she was a social climber.

Eleanor could no longer be the apple of her daddy's eye, so Caron had tossed her out. Or at least, ran her off for good.

Now, it was obvious she'd been estranged from her father all these years. But she'd found a way back in. Maybe.

Nico studied the grainy picture again, deciding this little girl looked a lot like his woman in red. But she also had the same features as Security Ellie. And after that, it didn't take much to put the pieces of the puzzle together.

Had the princess returned to claim her kingdom?

Chapter Twelve

ELEANOR WORE HER own hair today. But she had it braided and twisted in a bun to make her look like a schoolmarm. She'd also added her big black glasses to highlight that, putting in low prescription green contacts. She wore a sweeping midi-skirt in deep blue with buttery-soft baseball tan ankle boots and a crisp white blouse and pearls. For some strange reason, she'd begun to enjoy playing dress up again. In spite of working long hours to establish security for the upcoming Valentine's party at the estate and discreetly inquiring into the stores accounts and her father's condition, she still was glad to be back at Castle's.

It could be the exquisite clothes Tiffany and she had fun buying. Or it could be the twenty pounds gone and the strong, healthy body she'd worked years to hone.

Maybe it was being back here inside the department store where glamour and beauty assaulted her at every turn.

Or perhaps all of this had something to do with the man stalking the hallways like a big cat on the prowl. Nico Lamon haunted her dreams, and filled her head with images she needed to forget. How long had he been there yesterday when she'd stood looking at the mural? What did he think he knew about her? Why did he make her feel like being less of a guard and more of a woman?

Her heart quickened at that thought.

Johnny came into her office. "Boss, you need to see this." He handed Eleanor a full-page ad from the Dallas paper.

She looked at the captioned picture and gasped.

The caption read—*Has anyone seen the Lamon Lady? Why is she so elusive?*

The photo was a replica of Nico and her, but obviously with models. The handsome dark-headed man knelt to place a red satin pump on the blonde woman's foot while they looked into each other's eyes. The caption invited customers to come into Castle's and try on their own pair of Lamon shoes.

Eleanor took it all in, memories washing over her in a heated rush. She almost wished she could be the woman depicted in that one perfect moment. But that would never work.

"Oh, my," she said, glancing up at Johnny. "His marketing department didn't waste any time, did they?"

Johnny grinned. He looked dapper as always in a gray suit and bright red tie with one white heart centered on it. Everyone got into the Valentine's spirit around here during the season. "No, but when you're just *you*, this model looks a lot like *you*."

Eleanor tried to clear her head. "Then she can be his spokesperson. I have too much to take care of here."

Johnny poured a cup of coffee. "Did you find out more about your daddy?"

"Yes," she said, wishing she didn't have to be so cloak-

and-dagger. "He has dementia, but Caron is keeping that a big secret while she has him signing papers and contracts and transferring money and property." Then she added, "My sources tell me my father is being cared for, but Caron could have the doctors in her pocket, too." Eleanor had called in some markers and gotten a thorough report. "I did find out he has round-the-clock nurses and doctors who come and go, but who knows what they're prescribing for him?"

Johnny looked skeptical. "Claude visits him now and then. I'll ask him how your dad's doing and report back to you."

"Thank you."

Johnny rubbed a hand down his five o'clock shadow. "She's had some heavy-hitting lawyers in and out of her office."

"She somehow finagled power of attorney when he first showed signs of being sick," Eleanor replied. "I've got some high-powered lawyers of my own discreetly checking into that, and I have HR and accounting pulling files per inventory concerns and shoplifting. But I have to be very careful. People talk, and I can't risk anyone finding out until I have all the facts in place. It takes time to build a case, and I don't have much time."

Johnny tapped his fingers on the desk. "Hey now, you have your ways. Frankly, a lot of people here know Caron is shifty. Enough said, okay?"

"Okay. Thank you, Johnny, for your discretion, as well as for helping me with security preparations for the Valentine's party."

A knock pounded at the closed door. Johnny stood and opened it. "Hello, Mr. Lamon," he said with an exaggerated tone. "Something we can do for you?"

"I need to talk to Ellie. In private."

Eleanor gulped a breath, but then spoke to Johnny. "It's fine."

Nico came into the room, wearing a tweed jacket, jeans, and dark leather boots. After taking his time scrutinizing her in a way that made Eleanor either want to kiss him or get out of this tiny room, he said, "You look different today."

"Colored contacts," she replied. "Like to keep people on their toes."

He glanced at the paper on her desk. "You've seen the first ad?"

"Yes," she replied, careful to keep her features neutral as her gaze fluttered to the couple in the picture. "Very striking."

"There will be at least three more. One in Sunday's paper. Another one the Friday before the Valentine's party at the Castle estate."

"Thanks for alerting me."

He pushed at his hair. "You know, since you're so good at disguises, I had a thought."

Eleanor's heart did a nervous spin. Grabbing her water bottle, she asked, "What kind of thought?"

His smile held a dare. "What if you disguised yourself as our missing Lamon Lady and did a few rounds of PR with me?"

Eleanor almost choked on the sip of water she'd taken.

After a brief coughing fit, she shook her head. "I don't think that would be wise."

"You mean because you're obviously undercover here? Possibly investigating the woman at the helm?"

So he still thought she was Ellie the security guard, deep undercover because of Caron. A slip of relief moved through Eleanor. He might not know everything after all.

"Well, yes, possibly, but I can't discuss that with you. But what you're suggesting would be a conflict of interest."

He shook his head. "I think it would be in the best interest—for both of us. We each need certain things to happen. I've been stalling with these mysterious ads, but if we presented you in such a way that everyone can get a glimpse here and there, it would heighten the illusion and the fantasy, don't you think?"

"So I'd be a decoy or a stand-in for the real Lamon Lady?"

"Yes, exactly."

Eleanor took in a breath. Was he bribing her or blackmailing her? She couldn't be sure of either.

"Why don't you use this model?" she asked, pinning her finger against the ad. "She's really pretty."

"I like you better. Besides, you're here and so good at becoming someone new every day. Makes sense, too, for security purposes. We'd be shooting around the store, so you can still be undercover."

"But ... the employees will know it's me."

"I don't think they'll notice. I mean, I have the upmost confidence in your abilities." He went on as if it were a done deal. "I'd also like to do some ads away from the city at my mother's ranch in Ft. Worth."

"You are seriously kidding, right?"

"No. I'm *serious*. I'd like you to cover for us until the real woman steps forward. Or at least until after this big party is over."

"And what if I don't agree to this?'

"Why wouldn't you?"

"Because it's a bit ambitious."

"I'm a bit ambitious myself. This is a proposition, and you'd be doing me a favor. I really need to save face and keep the momentum going." He glanced around at the monitors and video machines. "You should certainly understand that."

Eleanor decided this room needed to be renovated so things weren't so cramped and tight. She could easily reach out and touch his face, run her fingers through his hair. Except that the man was toying with her. She refused to crack.

She couldn't come clean now. She had too much at stake. And maybe he knew that.

"I'm not so sure about this," she admitted. "How long do you plan on fooling people?"

"As long as it takes," he said. "All of these disguises, Ellie. Are they to throw off would-be criminals, Caron Castle, or me?"

Eleanor's pulse dropped right along with her expectations.

"Nico, why are you really here?"

"I'm trying to make a deal with you. But hear me out

before you become even more indignant, please."

"Talk," she said. "I have lots to do today."

"All you have to do is show up at a few functions. Disguised, of course."

"I told you I can't do that. I'm not your lady person."

"I'll ask no questions, and you don't have to give answers," he said. "This campaign is on a roll with the customers. It's become a social media frenzy. Everyone wants to see you, be you, or at least find you."

Eleanor got up. "Not me. Her. And I'm not her. You need to get out of my office."

He stood and took her hand. "Listen to me. You'd only need to pretend … until Valentine's night at the party."

She almost fainted. That was her exact plan—to pretend until the party where she would expose Caron in front of everyone. But he'd somehow wrestled it away from her for his own selfish purposes. She'd have to reveal herself to him, too.

"I can't possibly be someone I'm not. I'll be working security at that party." And trying to rescue her father.

"You can do your job," he said, his expression relaxed, his eyes full of expectation. "Acting as my spokesperson gives you carte blanche to the estate. You'll be able to wander around, talking to everyone there."

Had he read her mind? Talked to someone who'd finally caved and told him her sad, tragic story?

"Ellie, all I need you to do is show up for a few functions and move through the room. You don't have to introduce yourself. Just do your graceful, beautiful thing and leave.

Then we'll take you to a very private place to get some shots for the ads."

"Stop," she said, her heart hurting. "You don't understand. I can't do that."

He pressed on. "I do have an ulterior motive."

Hah! She knew it. "And what's that, Nico?"

"I want to spend more time with you. This is a perfect way to make that happen without riling the dragon queen."

She wanted to be with him, too. But not this way.

"But you do understand, the real *me* is not the woman you saw running away."

His gaze slipped over her in a slow, intimate way. "No, you're not the type to run from a challenge. You have courage and you're here under pressure, trying to do the right thing." He held her hands to his lips, brushing a kiss over her knuckles. "Traits I admire and appreciate. And understand."

Eleanor looked into his eyes and saw the truth. He knew who she was, but he wasn't going to make her admit it. Was he trying to help her and protect her, in his own charming, confused way?

Her heart and her head warred with wanting to ask him outright and needing to deny everything between them. She had too much at stake to trust him right now.

But he had her backed into a corner. "If I don't agree to this, are you going to expose my investigation?"

"No," he said, honesty in that one word. "No, I wouldn't do that to you. You need your job, and I need … this one favor."

He leaned so close she thought he was going to kiss her. "I'm taking advantage of the situation, same as you."

Eleanor's heart hardened again, but she couldn't risk anyone else knowing her true identity and why she was here. "I'll show up to your events, Nico, and I'll play coy and pretend to be the woman you seem so intent on making me, but once the Valentine's party is over, you'll need to either end this campaign or find another Lamon Lady." She looked him in the eye. "Because the woman you met at the gala is not coming back."

"I understand," he said, shaking her hand in a businesslike manner. His eyes, though, held a high hope and a bit of enchantment. "You won't regret this, Ellie. I promise."

"I already regret it," she replied. "It's a farfetched idea, but ... I do love my disguises." She'd show him, all right.

He let go of her hands and touched a finger to her hair.

"You are very good at disguising who you really are, Ellie. I hope you won't lose yourself in all those brilliant illusions. Because, truly, I'd love to meet the real woman underneath this façade."

And with that, he turned and headed toward the door. "I'll be in touch."

AFTER NICO LEFT, Eleanor pulled up the files she'd been gathering on Caron Robertson Smith Castle. She tried to refocus on what she'd found, so she could add more articles and papers to the electronic dossier.

But she couldn't stop thinking about Nico and what she'd just agreed to do. Disguise herself as the Lamon Lady.

Why did he have to come back now, when she'd plotted and planned out every detail of this undercover persona, when she was so close to having enough information on Caron to end her reign over Castle's forever?

A much more exiting subject.

She was about to call him and tell him she'd reconsidered when her cell phone rang.

"Tiffany, what's up?"

"We have a very special visitor in the cosmetic department," Tiffany said. "Nico Lamon's mother just arrived. Remember Joan Collins in Dynasty?"

Eleanor's heart did a spin of panic. Nico had a mother. Of course he did. She'd read up on his family. "Yes, why?"

"Well, Lila Lamon makes that woman look plain and dull. You have to see this. She's got a dog and an entourage. And well … I think she's planning on staying in Dallas for a while."

NICO WASN'T PLEASED.

His mother. In Dallas.

"I thought she was in the South of France," he said into the phone to Mira as he and Caron headed back to the store after doing an hour-long local television show where they'd cooked, talked about fashion, and made suggestions on romantic Valentine's dinners.

"She flew in under the radar," Mira replied.

Nico headed up the elevator from the parking garage. Turning to Caron, he said, "My mother is here. Her timing is not good."

"Well, I'm glad she's here." Caron snorted beside him. "You know, if we had our spokesperson, I wouldn't have had to fill in on that two-bit local television hour."

Nico faced Caron with a frown. "You seemed to be a natural in front of the cameras, Caron. I think you won over the audience with your charm and candor."

"Really?" she said, preening. It only took a couple of compliments to put the woman right back into her own self-involved vortex.

"Really," he retorted, remembering how she'd managed to edge out both the host and him during the cooking segment. And to put her in a good mood, he added, "I'm happy to report I've located the Lamon Lady. I hope to meet with her privately later today."

That stopped Caron in her Louboutins. "Why not bring her here so I can talk to her and give her a piece of my mind?"

"She's a very private person. She's willing to work with us, but under her terms."

Caron's steam puffed down. "Well, that's more like it as long as the terms include doing her job."

The elevator opened. Mira was waiting, her day book and cell in her hands.

"Have Mrs. Lamon meet us in my office," Caron said to Mira on a dismissive note.

Mira, who really didn't take orders from anyone, replied, "She's down on the floor, sampling perfume. We'll meet her there."

Nico had been caught between these two since he'd left Ellie's office earlier to hurry away with Caron. And now he had his beloved mother to contend with, too. He felt a headache coming on.

But when the elevator opened and they were about to march over to greet his mother, he caught sight of his favorite person.

Security Ellie hurried down the wide aisle between the shoe department and the perfume counter, her skirt swaying against her hips and her boots a bit naughty compared to the rest of her outfit. She looked proper, so very proper.

Which made him think not so proper thoughts.

His mood brightened considerably when she turned and saw him. He would stick with his plan and hope she'd open up to him. She made him laugh and challenged him, and he never quite knew which Ellie he might see. She was a real woman who took care of things without all the squawking and nitpicking. Mysterious and down to earth. He wanted to find *his* Ellie, and he really hoped his Security Ellie would walk down those stairs wearing red one day.

She turned off to head toward the accessories department. He wanted to follow her, but then he heard his mother. "Nico!"

Lila Lamon greeted him with a smile and the clatter of diamonds and pearls falling across her neck, hands, and arms. Her tiny white dog made shrill woof sounds that sounded more like a suffering mouse.

"Mother. How good to see you."

"Nico, darling, where have you been? I'm famished, and Gigi needs her nap. We will check into my suite at the Omni, right after you take me to a very late lunch so I don't faint from hunger."

Drenched in *Luscious*, the iconic floral Lamon fragrance that women wore the world over, she kissed him and then patted his cheeks, her silver-gray eyes giving him a hard stare. "You look tired, darling."

"Mother, why are you here?"

"You could say hello and give me a hug before the interrogation."

Nico hugged her close, loving her in spite of her overbearing ways. "Hello, Mother. What are you doing here?"

"I came to see you, of course," his mother said, her cream leather jacket crinkling right along with her eye makeup. Gigi recognized Nico, immediately trying to jump out of her white patent leather doggie carrier with the Lamon L engraved on its side.

"That's wonderful, but I'm very busy with this ad campaign."

"So I hear," Lila said, smiling at Mira. His assistant had always kept his mother up to date.

Lila's slick silver symmetric bob fell forward. "I hear you seem to have lost the one who fit the shoes."

"But I've found her again," Nico said, grinning. "I'm meeting her today. Alone."

All three women started talking at once.

Nico saw a woman approaching them—one who took his breath away.

Security Ellie had changed. She now wore a winter white wool suit—fitted jacket with skinny pants, a single strand of gleaming pearls, and ... red shoes. Not *the* red shoes, but Lamon's, all the same. She carried a white clutch with one lone red heart at the clasp. From the Lamon collection.

Her lips were a fiery red, too. Her hair was down, but in an elegant sweep-over. Her eyes were blue again, full of a determination that kind of scared him. What was she up to?

"Excuse me," he said. Managing to extract himself from the Bermuda Triangle, he tuned out the women clamoring for information and met her in the middle of the aisle.

"What are you doing?"

She gave him a brilliant smile. "I'm reporting for duty, Mr. Lamon. How am I doing so far?"

Nico didn't have words, but he took in a breath and then let it out. "I think you've nailed it. But ... what's your plan?"

"I plan to leave this department store on your arm, and take you away to a marvelously private place."

He liked that idea, but he was still afraid of her motives.

"To talk or commit murder?"

Her now-icy blue eyes pinned him. "I haven't decided yet."

"I see," he said, out of breath again. "Shall we go then?"

She sent him a covert stare. The woman knew how to throw him off. "Not until I meet your mother."

Enough. Nico took her hand before dragging her to a corner between scarves and wraps. "I don't know if that's a good idea. She's with Caron and Mira."

"I know. If I can fool those three, I can fool anyone, right?"

Security Ellie had taken this assignment to new heights.

"You do have a point, but … are you sure?"

"I'm ready. Are you?"

"I need help escaping," he replied. "I just need a couple of hours of peace away from this store and shoes and people clamoring for my attention, and especially away from Caron, my mother, and my assistant. Let's just leave now, please. You can meet my mother later."

She hesitated and then … something turned warm in her cool gaze.

"Come with me." She took him by the hand, then led him to the service stairs that went to the garage.

Chapter Thirteen

SHOVING HIM INTO a sleek black sports car, Ellie glanced around the garage. "Johnny is covering for a couple of hours, but then I have to get back."

"Of course." Nico loved the studious, serious way she did her job. "Is this your car?"

"No, it's a rental I had delivered earlier. Something the Lamon Lady would drive, don't you think?"

He studied her features while she drove a tad too fast through the garage.

A pert nose. Ivory skin that shimmered with a soft glow. Full lips. And those eyes—cobalt and luminous.

This had to be his Lamon Lady, his woman in red, his Ellie. He couldn't see it any other way. Maybe today while they were alone, he could find out the truth.

"Are you kidnapping me?" he teased, the excitement of their escape staying with him.

She checked traffic and then spun out of the garage. "You asked for my help."

"I did, but now I'm wondering if that was wise on my part. Where are we going?"

"You'll see."

The little car purred along I-35 and merged with I-30,

heading northeast. Dallas sprawled behind them, vast and shining in tones of gray and silver.

The crisp February weather didn't allow for putting the top down, but Nico was almost glad. It meant he was closed off in this go-cart of a vehicle with a woman who kept him guessing.

A woman who could shift gears as fast as her little car.

"Are you taking me to your lair?"

"I don't have a lair."

"Okay, your tower?"

"I don't have a tower."

"Where do you live?"

"None of your business."

He laughed at that, and tried again. "Do you like your job?"

"I do, and I can't afford to lose it," she said, sincerity ringing in the tight space between them. "I have degrees in both business and criminal investigation, with security courses on the side. I've worked undercover before, but never in such an elegant manner."

Nico wanted to ask her more, but he was afraid too many questions would break the delicate thread woven between them.

He wanted her to fill in the gaps for him. It was then he realized she was playing a very dangerous game—a game he'd forced on her.

If this woman was who he thought she was, it explained why she wouldn't want this kind of exposure when she was trying to stay undercover. And what had he done? He'd dragged her right into the bright spotlight she'd tried to avoid.

People called him ruthless, but that was part of being in a competitive, cutthroat business. He couldn't be ruthless about Ellie, though. His heart had gone soft the moment he'd met her. *Both times*.

If he were a drinking man, he could sure use a drink right now. The Ellie mystery was driving him nuts.

When she turned off the freeway, he saw the signs for the Dallas Arboretum and Botanical Gardens. "What is this?"

"It's like Central Park but in Dallas," she explained. "People picnic here, go bike riding or fishing, and canoeing out on White Lake, outdoors things. There are turtles and birds of all kinds, even white pelicans."

"You seem to know this place well," he said, hoping she would finally open up to him.

"I used to come here with my parents. A long, long time ago."

The wistful tone in her words tore through him. He knew in his heart this was his Ellie, come back to claim the life she'd lost. She was the perfect example of the Lamon Lady, a smart, capable working woman who didn't put up with anyone's bunk. But he also knew he couldn't push her, that he had to let her do this her way.

Or he'd lose her. And he didn't want to lose her. He didn't care about the spokesperson part. She was the Lamon Lady, through and through. His Lamon Lady. A woman who could keep up with him and probably surpass him. He needed to know her history, to understand what drove her.

She parked the car and turned to him. "There's a nice path around the lake. Want to go for a walk?"

"I'd love that. Fresh air always makes me feel better about things."

She laughed, elegance in every tone. "That and … I had someone tip off the Dallas paper that the Lamon Lady might be here today for a photo shoot."

Nico hurried around the car and held her door, then gave her his hand to help her out. When she didn't protest, he smiled at her. And she smiled back.

ELEANOR COULDN'T BELIEVE she'd done this—dressed up like the Lamon Lady and left work. Well, she did have a lunch hour and Johnny would take care of things. If Caron found out …. No, she was through worrying about Caron. Eleanor had a whole team gathering everything she needed to press charges against Caron Castle. Possible embezzlement and forgery, and if all the facts added up, a shoplifting ring, too.

Longing to tell Nico the truth, she knew she couldn't. Not yet, not until she knew her father and Castle's were both safe. For now, she only wanted to bask in the crisp air and the warm sun and walk along the lake where her parents used to bring her.

And she wanted to make sure the cameras lurking in the bushes captured a good image of Nico Lamon with the Lamon Lady.

If she had to play games, she'd play on her own terms. This place brought her peace. The Lamon Lady would love this place. And the Lamon Lady would take advantage of the situation she'd been forced into.

For a couple of hours, she would pretend. She would spend time with this man who kept her confused and on high alert. Not necessarily a prince, but close. So close.

"Why did you do this?" he asked now, the sound of geese and ducks fussing out on the water. "Since you didn't seem too keen to my idea."

She shrugged. "I decided this was an opportunity. I might live to regret my rash decision once our images are plastered in the paper. But … you asked a favor. I might need a favor of my own in return."

Nico placed a hand to his heart. "Oh, and here I thought I'd finally won you over."

Eleanor put on the Lamon Lady face, cool and confident. "Are you trying to win me over?"

"Would you let me?"

"I don't know how to answer that," she said, some of her insecurities returning. "I come with a lot of baggage."

"I don't mind that. I travel with women who always have a lot of baggage."

He did have a wit about him.

"But their baggage is designer."

"And you are one of a kind."

Eleanor basked in his kind words. Stopping by a bench, she whirled to stare at him. "Who are you saying that to, Nico? Ellie in security or your fantasy woman?"

He laughed, reaching to grasp her hand. "Both," he said. "You're both helping me avoid three demanding women."

"Are you Macbeth?" she asked with a playful grin.

"No, but they are definitely the Weird Sisters."

"So Caron, your mother, and Mira are a bit too much?"

"Your insight is amazing."

She started strolling again, the warmth of his hand holding hers doing funny things to her heart. "It didn't take much to see the panic in your eyes earlier. You latched onto me a tad too quickly."

He stopped her again, angling his body towards her. "That's because you came along at exactly the right time. I wanted to see you anyway."

"Why?" She sensed he wanted to say more, and she had to wonder just how much more he knew about her. But she wasn't about to tell him anything else.

"Why?" He looked into her eyes with such hope Eleanor felt herself slipping. "You're interesting. You're so smart—part diva and part spy—and you surprise me every day." He stood back to survey her form, still holding her hands. "The disguises intrigue me."

Basking in the warmth and sincerity of his words, she said, "The disguises are the easy part."

"Who are you hiding from?"

Flustered, she pulled away. "It's part of my job. If I look the same every day, shoplifters will notice and learn to skirt around me."

"Why didn't you give chase at the gala the other night?" he asked. "If you were watching on the monitors, you could have helped."

A trick question. Eleanor took her time in answering it. "I needed to keep the visual, to help Johnny. He knew what he was doing, and he followed proper protocol."

"So you trust your staff?"

"Completely."

"But you don't trust Caron Castle?"

That question stopped her cold since she was pretty sure Caron had people watching her. What if Nico was one of those people, and this had all been a set-up? "Do you?"

"No, not really."

"Why are you doing business with her?"

Nico's dark eyebrows shot up before his expression changed to a resolved frown. "I'm doing business with Castle Department Store. My father had a lucrative account with Castle's many years ago. After he died, we lost the account and almost lost our business."

Eleanor remembered reading about that. She also thought about their very quick but forgettable encounter. Forgettable for him, at least.

"But you brought it back."

"Yes, by going back to all the retailers and distributors to show them the House of Lamon was still alive and viable. I personally helped with creating a new, modern line of women's clothes—and shoes that matched anything from Louboutin or Manolo Blahnik. It took a whole team of people, but we did it. We made it back to the top."

"So you really love what you do?"

"Yes, of course." He gazed over the water where two colorful paddleboats passed by, the teens inside laughing and chattering away. "I didn't for a long time. I spent my father's hard-earned money and wasted away at college, barely passing, traveled the world on yachts and private planes with women I didn't really respect or care about. But one day, I woke up alone and hungover, and I heard a voicemail on my phone. My father was ill and dying."

"So you went home."

He gave her a look of understanding while they stood underneath a towering oak. "I went home, and I promised him on his deathbed that I would make things right. That's what family is all about, don't you think?"

Eleanor's heart beat so fast she thought she might lose her breath. He'd done the same thing she was trying to do, but he hadn't had to hide in secrecy. But what if she told him the truth and he went straight to Caron? What would she do then?

Wanting to pour her heart out to him, she instead glanced at her watch. "I … I need to get back. I don't want to lose my job."

"I'm sorry," he said, holding her there. "I want you to understand, Ellie, if you need me for anything, I'm here."

She weighed the sincerity of that statement against the fear in her heart. "But you won't always be here. And that's what I need to remember."

She turned and hurried back up the path to her car. Then she remembered the photographer she'd planted. What kind of image would she see in the paper?

Chapter Fourteen

NICO HAD PUSHED her too far. He'd reminded her of the very reason she'd come home. She'd been tossed aside and abandoned by the father who'd doted on her when she was young. He certainly knew how she felt. He'd been a prodigal, shunning his father's advice to live it up while his family struggled.

He hurried behind her. "Ellie?"

But she didn't turn around. She didn't need to. He knew the truth, and he hurt for her. But he wanted her to trust him enough to tell him. How could he help her?

Suddenly, it became clear to him what he needed to do.

He needed to show her that she could count on him, no matter what.

He got in the car, watching her shaky movements. "I didn't mean to upset you."

"I'm fine. I just need to stay focused on my job. And I believe I completed part of my favor to you today."

"Wait," he said, his hand gentle on hers. "Listen to me."

"What's there to listen to, Nico?" she said. "This is a flirtation for you, an escape, something to do because you're bored, right?"

"I'm not bored," he retorted, anger making his denial

sharp. "I'm passionate about my work, Ellie. I want to make beautiful things for women. My father was the same. To say I'm using you because I'm bored is an insult to everything I've created."

"I'm sorry," she said, "but I don't understand what's happening."

Calming down, he touched a hand to her face. "I want to be with you when I should be searching for the woman who left the gala. This whole campaign hinges on finding her, but I'd rather be here, getting to know the woman who's right in front of me. That's the honest truth. Frankly, it surprises me to feel this way."

Seeing the moisture forming in her eyes, he moved his hand up to catch one single teardrop against his finger. "Do you understand what I'm saying?"

She bobbed her head. "Yes, but I work in security, Nico. We're from different worlds. I can't be someone I'm not."

He held his hand to her neck. "Are we really so different?"

"I need to get back to work," she said, the grit in those words telling him she didn't want to go back so soon.

Taking a different approach, he used the only tactic he had left. He pulled her head around and kissed her, his lips settling over hers with an intent that held no boredom but carried the fire of his passion.

When he pulled away, awe filling his heart, he whispered, "I'm not playing. I'm serious."

Ellie's eyes misted over with a hue of emotions that took his breath away. Shock, confusion, fear, and longing, and maybe a little bit of hope. "You kissed me."

"Yes, and I enjoyed it. Very much."

Holding tight to the steering wheel, she said, "This can't be happening."

"Why not?"

"We don't match."

"Our lips matched up perfectly. Want me to show you again?"

Her nod was barely a movement, just enough to give him hope. So he brought her closer and kissed her several more times, his mind filling with the need to hold her and protect her. But would she let him do that? Would she let him into the world she'd stayed hidden inside for so long?

Ellie ended the kisses, her lips pink and swollen, her eyes filled with regret and resolve. "I didn't get to show you the white pelicans."

That statement held a finality that broke Nico's heart. "We can come back one day."

"I don't think so."

She straightened her mussed hair, and then cranked the car. They rode in silence for a few moments before she said, "Maybe you can do me a favor now?"

Crash the castle. Take down an army. Fall on his sword. "Anything."

"I need to get into the Valentine's party at the estate Saturday night, and I know you expect me to be there as the Lamon Lady."

Confused, he nodded. "As head of security, you're required to be there anyway, right?"

"Yes, but I'm not allowed to mingle with anyone or … go upstairs. We are to stay on the grounds and first floor only, and patrol the crowd from a distance. You know, see and not be seen. We have to guard the stairs."

"Oh, I get it. And you need to get inside and up close? You need to see something or someone upstairs at the Castle estate?"

Her eyes held his, an understanding passing between them. "Yes. I'll need a gown. The most exquisite gown you can find."

"I will design you a gown," he promised, his head already filling with ideas. "In return, you will appear as the Lamon Lady."

"Yes, that's the agreement. I want to look the part, but we don't have much time."

Nico touched his hand to her still-wet cheeks. "There is always time to design a masterpiece, *bella*."

ELEANOR HURLED HERSELF out of the elevator, and rushed to the secret stairs to text Tiffany.

Turret Room. STAT.

There, she paced, worried, and kicked off her shoes. She had to do a quick change before getting out on the floor. Nico had kissed her. And she'd kissed him back. Oh, the man could kiss. This couldn't be real, but his lips on hers had felt real. Better than anything she'd ever imagined.

And now, she'd asked him to help her with a ploy that might not work. But how else could she get upstairs to see her father?

"I had no choice," Eleanor whispered while she headed to the turret room. Nico could get her in—as the Lamon Lady. Then he would parade her around. She'd ask to see the rest of the house, and Caron would be forced to allow that. Nico would insist on escorting her upstairs.

And hopefully, Caron would leave them alone.

She'd be dressed in one of his exquisite creations, but she hadn't specified the color. So she didn't know what she'd be wearing, but she would become the Lamon Lady, for Nico and for her own purposes. And then, this whole charade would finally be over.

Get in as the Lamon Lady, exit as head of security. With her father in tow, hopefully.

Caron would be furious, of course.

Tiffany texted back. "Be there in a while. I've been busy all morning escorting Thelma and Louise around the store."

Caron and Lila. A formidable pair.

Eleanor smiled at that. Tiffany knew her job, and she was good at everything from makeovers to soothing frazzled nerves.

Eleanor finished getting back into her work attire, deciding to take a minute to sink onto a dainty slipper stool to stare out the window. Nico had kissed her. And then he'd agreed to make her a dress that everyone would remember.

Which was good. Eleanor would reveal to Caron and all of her important guests exactly who she really was. Not a fantasy woman at all, but Eleanor Castle.

And then, she'd take over things from there.

She only had a few days to finish building a case against her stepmother. What else was Caron hiding?

Nico hadn't pressed for more on the ride back to downtown Dallas. Instead, he'd held her hand off and on, his gaze moving over her with an intensity that made Eleanor want more kisses.

But that couldn't happen again. She had too much at stake to sneak kisses in the park with a man who lived a world away from Texas. He'd go back to his world and she'd stay here, cleaning up the mess Caron had made of Charles Castle's legacy.

Lost in her thoughts on how to proceed, Eleanor jumped at a knock at the door. Tiffany rarely knocked since she usually used the side door that led to the employee area and the service exit, but with things so up in the air around here, maybe she was being overly cautious.

Eleanor got up to let her in.

But found Annabelle standing there instead.

"What are you doing?" Eleanor asked. She hardly saw Annabelle or Aidan. When she did, she tried to avoid them, so they wouldn't recognize her.

"You come in here a lot," Annabelle said, scooting inside and closing the door behind her. "Why is that?"

Eleanor laughed, waving a hand toward the few clothes hanging on a rack in the corner. "You caught me. I keep my security wardrobe in here. Easy to stay undercover that way."

Annabelle toyed with a heavy length of silver chains

weighing down her neck. "Does my mother know about this?"

"Yes, she signed off on it." Which was true. Caron had hurriedly signed off on several security measures Eleanor had sent to her as a test. She'd failed miserably, because she didn't care about security or how much money she was bleeding from the store each month.

"Cool," Annabelle said, heading to the rack. "I could use some new wardrobe pieces myself."

"These aren't for your use," Eleanor retorted, wondering just how much spying Annabelle did since she obviously didn't do much in the way of work. "Aren't you supposed to be in the accessories department?"

"I'm allowed two breaks per day."

"Right." Checking her watch, Eleanor hoped Tiffany didn't burst in ranting away. She didn't want to get her friend in trouble.

Annabelle's slender fingers played over the dresses and tunics. "Never mind. These are so old fogey."

"Old fogey?" Eleanor didn't think so. But then, she wasn't wearing black leather skinny jeans and a blood-red slouchy cashmere sweater that had broken hearts etched in white all over it. "What kind of fashion do you like?"

"Not the kind Nico Lamon designs," Annabelle offered. "My mother thinks he's going to fall head over heels with me, and then take me away to Italy or Paris. So not going to happen."

"Did you follow me up here?"

"No. But I see things and I watch people. I decided to

follow you on your rounds, you know, just for kicks."

"I see. You do know that I'm the head of security, right?"

"Yes, and you do know my mother, right?"

"Is that a threat?"

"No. It's a warning. She's a mess right now what with Mr. C being so sick and the store being barely pulled away from the brink of bankruptcy. And she's got you on her radar. She thinks I'm up here spying for her, just so you know."

Surprised at Annabelle's candor, Eleanor said, "Wow. I felt she had people watching me, but … sending her own daughter?"

"Yep," Annabelle replied. "A real mother of the year. I'm trying to stay out of her way. Today, she's got Nico's mother with her. It's scary times two."

Not anymore scary than your outfit, Eleanor wanted to add. But Annabelle did pull off goth-punk in a pretty good way, even if the tone of the hearts was sad.

"I'm not worried about your mother," Eleanor said. "I'm doing my job, but maybe she doesn't like that I've found some holes in our security."

"That and how you pressed charges against one of her best friend's son. I used to date him, so I know what he's been up to. He steals for the thrill even though his family has a pile of big Texas money."

"Well, he's stolen for the last time," Eleanor replied, anger coloring her words.

"He won't go to jail," Annabelle said. "His daddy hired some top-notch expensive lawyer. And the queen has already agreed to drop the charges."

Really mad now, Eleanor kept her cool. "I see. I'll have to discuss that with your mother."

"Good luck with that," Annabelle said. "You know, you remind me of someone."

"Oh, I get that a lot," Eleanor said, afraid she'd blow her cover. She'd have to go back to wigs.

"No, I mean it's somebody I know or maybe I've met. Maybe from school or possibly a nanny we had. We used to run off nannies on a weekly basis."

"I've never been a nanny, and I really need to get back to work. Why don't you get back, too, before your mother misses you?"

"I'll figure it out," Annabelle said, turning to leave. But first, she sauntered over to the rack and uncoiled a gray silk scarf. "I'm going to borrow this. But I'll bring it back."

Eleanor blocked the door. "You'd better, or I'll have to bring *you* in."

Annabelle's look of utter surprise was priceless. She probably never had anyone reprimand her before. "Okay, then. I see you're serious about your job."

"That's what I get paid for."

Annabelle twisted the scarf around her neck with a deliberate flair. "I'll figure out where I've seen you before. Once I do, we'll talk again."

Eleanor let out a held breath. The sooner she got through this and revealed her real identity, the better off she'd be.

But then, the real work would begin.

And, Nico would be gone.

The side door opened, and Tiffany slipped in. "What's up?"

"You won't believe it," Eleanor said. "I'm going to the ball again. And I need you to be my fairy godmother."

"I'm in," Tiffany said with a knowing grin. "All in."

Chapter Fifteen

"I NEED YOU to come to my hotel suite."

Eleanor stared up at Nico. She checked behind them, his request dancing like a lost shiver down her spine. "What do you mean?"

He'd caught her in a hallway that led to the credit department on the second floor, where a line of customers stood waiting for service on returns and to pay their bills. Beyond that was the popular *Castle's Chocolates* counter, where Tiffany bought luscious truffles for them to share in the turret room, and the Castle Café, where delicious breakfast and lunch menus kept shoppers coming back. Her father had cleverly put the chocolate counter between the credit and lingerie departments, so even disgruntled shoppers could leave happy with either chocolate or frilly intimate garments. If a shopper had a problem that wasn't corrected to their satisfaction, they received a free box of Castle truffles on the way out. Most came back.

At least Caron had not ended that policy, mainly because, according to Tiffany, when she'd tried, the employees and the loyal customers had revolted in a big way.

Nico laughed and winked, bringing Eleanor back from her thoughts. "I need to do a fitting. I've drawn a gown, and

I had my assistant find a reputable fabric store to buy the fabric. Blue chiffon, to match your eyes. But unlike with the clothes we've been showing and selling here, I can't fit you in the main fitting salon the way I would with a client."

"For obvious reasons," she said, her pulse doing little Valentine-like scribbles through her system.

"Yes, and because I want to be alone with you."

Alone? Eleanor wondered how she'd pull this off. "I have to finish my shift," she said. "Maybe tonight."

"Tonight is good. We'll order room service."

"This isn't a date, is it?"

Because that sure sounded like a line.

"It could be if you come incognito, as the Lamon Lady. But ... a working date," he replied, his gaze moving along her body as if he were already measuring and accessing. Maybe stripping away her defenses, too.

Her nerves tingled and sizzled. "Where? What time?"

"The Omni, seven o'clock?"

"Will your mother be there?"

"Goodness, no. She has a suite on the other end of the hotel, and I think she has plans to go to the symphony." He touched Eleanor's arm. "I'll have assistants there who will cut and sew around the clock—discreet ones who will not speak about what we're doing. We'll do the final fitting on Friday night before the party."

"That soon. An original Lamon gown in six days?"

"I'm that good," he said, his words husky, his breath warm. "And I love the auburn shag wig, by the way."

Eleanor looked into his eyes, remembering his lips on

hers. Her breath caught, and that sweet sensation that always took over her soul whenever he was around worked its magic on her again.

And that was how Caron and his mother found Eleanor and Nico when they came around the corner, talking quietly to each other.

And they both had today's paper in their hands.

"Well, what have we here?" Lila Lamon stopped on her black pumps, staring at her son. "Who is this lovely creature you seem to be about to ravage?"

Caron stomped forward in her knee-high tan boots. "That … is our security department manager, who shouldn't be bothering your son while he's trying to mingle with some of our top clients."

She shoved the paper at Nico, her expression shrewd. "I see you did meet in private with the Lamon Lady. But obviously not private enough."

Nico took the paper. He hadn't even had time to read it. But the pictures he saw did more for his promotion than any ad ever could. "How delightful."

Eleanor pretended no interest. But he angled the page so she could see the photos. "Look at that."

The photographer had captured them while he was standing away from Eleanor but holding both her hands. Her face was hidden, but she looked elegant and fashionable. She fit the mode of the woman everyone wanted to see. And they looked like a couple trying not to fall in love.

"Stunning," his proud mother said, holding up her own copy. "This is all the talk, darling. Did she agree to finally show herself at the Valentine's party next weekend?"

"She did, indeed," Nico said.

There were two other shots. In all of them, Eleanor's face was away from the camera. She'd obviously planned things that way.

Caron grabbed the paper back. "She should be at this show today."

Nico glanced at Eleanor. "I can't predict that. She has a busy schedule. But this photo will inspire our shoppers, no doubt."

Caron shot him a smoldering glare. "That white suit has already sold out in most of our stores. She'd better be at my party or … or … I don't know what I'll do."

Ignoring Caron, Nico said, "Mother, this is Ellen Sheridan. We were going over the details about the party at the Castle estate. The security team will handle crowd control."

Lila's shrewd gaze moved over Eleanor with a keen interest. "You're quite lovely yourself. I like your printed skirt and black cashmere sweater."

"Thank you," Eleanor said. "It's nice to meet you."

"She goes overboard with the disguises," Caron pointed out, her frown indicating she was not happy with the staff fraternizing with one of their fashion moguls. "But today, she looks downright plain."

Nico's eyes went dark. Too dark.

"You're right," Eleanor said before he could play the knight in shining armor. "I downplayed my makeup, purposefully wearing this old sweater and skirt so I could blend in."

"You're still a rare beauty," Lila said, her eyes on Nico, not Eleanor. "I'll look forward to seeing you at the party."

"Our security people will be out of sight," Caron said with a pasty smile. "Protocol, of course."

"What a shame," Lila retorted, her tone neutral.

Then she gave Nico a quick motherly kiss. "We shall talk later, my son."

"I'll be downstairs in five," Nico said. "The models know their jobs, and Mira is in charge until I get down there. Don't worry, Mrs. Castle, I'll charm all of your friends into buying our beautiful spring coats."

"I'll hold you to that," Caron said on a soft hiss. Darting a suspicious glare at Eleanor, she frowned. "And you, go and do something, please." Turning on her heel, she stormed away, Nico's mother beside her.

Eleanor turned to leave, but Nico grabbed her arm. "Don't let her get to you."

"She's not my worry," Eleanor replied, thinking the opposite. "I do my job, and I've shown the entire board that our security needs updating. She's angry because I've pressed charges against her friend's jewel-stealing son and made her look bad. Next, I start searching for the missing money she's possibly hiding in a Swiss bank."

"Do you believe she's been embezzling money?"

"I'm very close to proving it, yes."

"Ellie, be careful," he said. "Let me help you."

"You are helping me," she replied, realizing she'd said too much. "By dressing me."

Nico's eyebrows shot up at that. "I'd love nothing better." Sighing, he checked his watch. "I need to go and so do you."

He turned and headed for the stairs, taking them two at a time to get down to the women's fashion department.

Eleanor sent an SOS to Tiffany. Within minutes, they had her dressed as the Lamon Lady. She wore a bright red wool trench coat and dark sunglasses, tall black boots with slender three-inch heels, and a white cashmere scarf fashionably tied around her head, Grace Kelly style, that showed only a hint of her blonde hair.

"Go," Tiffany said after checking the hallway. Eleanor hurried to the trunk show, slowing to a ladylike speed as she moved to stand beside Nico.

When he tilted his head to see who had approached him, he seemed surprised, his eyes dancing over her and making her sweat in the heavy coat. "Are you walking?"

"I'm walking," she said. "Isn't that part of my job?"

"You're gorgeous," he whispered, sending her out after the last model had come back.

With no introductions at all, she wooed the crowd with her slight smile and mysterious air. The women seated around the catwalk went wild, cell phones flashing to get pictures. Eleanor did one turn before immediately retreating. The crowd chattered and buzzed, excited they'd just seen the Lamon Lady.

Nico decided she was very good at her job. And ... that she looked extremely good in red.

AFTER CHANGING, ELEANOR hurried up to the security office and let out a breath. This charade wasn't even really a charade anymore. She wondered who would out her first.

"I think I know who you are."

She whirled, a hand to her heart. Clearly, her skills were lacking these days. "Aidan?"

"Yes, and how do you know my name?" he asked with a raised brow. He pushed off a wall in the corner, sauntering toward her.

"How did you get in here?" she questioned to give herself time to recover.

"Johnny let me in. It's cool. I help out in security part-time."

"He did mention that."

"I thought it was time we met, officially."

"Yes, I make it a point to know everyone who works here. I have your file. You work in electronics."

He studied her face, his hazel eyes so like Annabelle's. "Annabelle and I have discussed you. We've noticed the way you try to disguise yourself."

"I like to play around with different wardrobes."

"So ... do you want to explain things to me?" Aidan asked, his dark hair falling across his brow in a tousled, bad-boy way.

"I don't owe you or anyone else any explanations," Eleanor replied, trying to keep her sanity. "I'm here to do a job, and that's all you need to know. So whatever else you'd like to say, spit it out and let me get back to work."

Aidan kept his dark eyes on her, his expression turning

from a smile to a frown. He was a handsome man, rugged and tanned, buff with a five o'clock shadow. He'd filled out, no longer the scrawny, awkward kid she remembered. He wore a denim jacket and washed-out jeans over black boots, but he looked fairly normal next to Annabelle's dark persona. Since he was the oldest, he was closer to Eleanor's age. Would he rat her out?

"Aidan, what do you want?"

"You're her, aren't you?"

Eleanor's entire system froze. Was this about to go down before she ever had a chance to see her father again? She couldn't risk that.

"Aidan—"

"You're the lady in red. That's where Annabelle and I saw you. At the gala. But you ran away, probably because you can't accept that spokesperson contract, right? I mean, you work here so that would be a conflict of interest."

She almost collapsed in relief. "Yes, but you can't tell anyone. I was undercover at the gala, and … I got caught up in a moment and couldn't stop it. It's a conflict of interest, of course. I had to leave. It's why I've been trying to disguise myself."

"Does anyone else know?"

Again, she chose her words carefully. "Johnny, of course. But no one else." She couldn't mention Tiffany.

"Now I know. I'll tell Annabelle so she'll keep her mouth shut."

"I'd appreciate that. Caron wouldn't be happy."

He started for the door. "Our mother doesn't care what

we do or how we do it, so we tend to become the friend of anyone who might be her enemy. Are you her enemy?"

"No, I work for the woman. But if she finds out about my little escapade, she'd surely fire me."

"Annabelle and I like you even though we don't know you. That's odd, don't you think?"

"A little."

He glanced at the monitors. "Oh, by the way, I'm pretty good at tech stuff. Yes, a geek and all of that. Johnny's called me up here before to check on glitches."

Eleanor wondered if he'd tried to find her on some of the daily videos. She'd been extra careful about ducking into the secret staircase. "That's good to know. Do you want to work security full time?"

"Not really. But I'd love to create a branch of Castle's that's dedicated to technology."

"Have you talked to your mother about this?"

"Are you kidding me? She wants me to become a doctor or lawyer."

"Did you go to college?"

"Yes, got a degree in technology and computer graphics, and now I'm stuck here. Sad for a twenty-seven-year-old man, right?"

"No. Not if you can parlay that into pushing your technology ideas."

"Here's hoping. I'll see you later. It was good to meet you." He gave her a grin and then left.

So now she'd talked to both of her siblings. They'd been comparing notes. Apparently, they'd each tried to feel her out, starting as spies for their mother but somehow warning Eleanor instead. Were they beginning to figure things out, too?

She couldn't wait for this to be over. But what if her father didn't recognize her? What if Caron had covered her tracks? And once this was over, where would that leave things with Nico and her?

Chapter Sixteen

AT 7:05 THAT evening, she knocked on the door of one of the bigger suites in the Omni Hotel. The executive suite was high in the sky. Eleanor's nerves seemed to be shooting that way, too.

Nico opened the door with a smile. "You came."

"We did have an appointment."

"Yes, but I was afraid you'd change your mind."

She'd certainly thought about doing just that. Her nerves were all jumbled and wired, and her emotions were doing a roller-coaster ride all over the place.

Why did the man have to look at her in a way that captured and freed her all at the same time?

He was casually dressed in jeans and a white shirt with the sleeves rolled up. That made her feel more relaxed since she'd worn jeans, boots, a sweater, and wrap. But his feet were bare. Something about him being barefooted made this more intimate.

"Do you want to come in?" he asked, that soft smile enticing her.

"I think so," she said. She edged around him, taking in the open wall that separated the bedroom from the sitting area. But the view caught her attention. "I've never been up this high."

She could see the entire city all lit up and sparkling, calling to her the same way his eyes and his lips did.

"Dallas is a stunning city," he said, escorting her into the sitting area where covered dishes were set out on the round table by the ceiling-to-floor windows. "I ordered dinner since I'm starving. I hope you don't mind."

Her appetite had slipped away around floor twenty or so. "No, I don't mind."

Candles burned on the table. Soft music played from somewhere. The lamps were muted, the atmosphere shouting seduction. "I thought this was a working night."

"It is," he said, pouring her a glass of sparkling water. "But one has to eat. And … I'm celebrating. That red coat you wore today sold out storewide in ten minutes. You're a star, Ellie."

"The Lamon Lady is a star. I'm just me."

"You are beautiful," he said, giving her space while his eyes drew her close.

Eleanor took a deep breath, accepting the compliment. "Maybe I should have my measurements done before I eat," she quipped.

His gaze did a stroll down her body. "I think you'll be fine."

After placing her purse and wrap on the high-backed sofa, she noticed the glass-encased fireplace that burned across a glistening bed of crystal rocks inside the wall. "It's cold out tonight."

"I know. The fire comes in handy."

He pulled out a chair, and Eleanor sat down. "I'm not used to such luxury, Nico."

"You should get used to it."

"Not on my salary. I spend extra on shoes, of course, but there isn't room in my budget for stuff like this."

His eyes held a message that indicated he'd like to spoil her, but he refrained from voicing the thought. "Let's eat. After, I'll call in my assistants. They're staying in the hotel, too."

"Do they get to eat dinner?"

"Of course."

The meal consisted of Texas standards—tender steak, loaded baked potatoes, and steamed vegetables, with decadent cheesecake for dessert.

While they ate, he asked her questions.

"Did you grow up in Dallas?"

"Yes."

"When did you move away?"

"When I was eighteen."

"What part did you live in?"

"We lived out from the city."

"Do you still have family here?"

"Yes."

"Are you ever going to tell me the truth?"

She stopped on that one, cocking her head. "That depends."

"On the dress? Or on me?"

"On what I came here to do."

"But you're not going to tell me everything tonight?"

"No."

Holding his water glass up, he regarded her with his heart in his eyes. "You realize I'm falling in love with you, don't you?"

Shock rolled through her, making her freeze. Lowering her head, she tried to get a hold of herself before lifting her gaze to him. "Nico, you aren't falling for me. You're searching for a woman who does not exit. She's your idea of perfection, but no woman can live up to that, not matter what she wears."

"My father used to say, 'It's not the clothes, it's the woman.' And Coco Chanel said, 'Fashion will come and go but style lasts forever'."

"Yes, I know that quote. My mother repeated it to me a lot. But … I'm not perfect. Neither is the woman you're searching for. Maybe she ran away because she knew she'd never measure up to your standards."

"Or maybe she ran away because she was afraid to have her heart broken," he replied, his hand reaching for hers. "I didn't see her as perfect, Ellie. I just saw her as perfect for me."

Eleanor pushed away from the table, making her voice remote. "Call your assistants, please. We should get to work."

Nico stood, approaching her. He hesitated for a moment, but firmly took her into his arms. She stayed stiff as he looked at her half-eaten food. "You didn't enjoy your meal?"

"I ate," she replied. "Thank you. The food was wonderful."

"We still have dessert."

"Maybe later," she said, softening enough to mold her body to his. She wished she could stay here with him for a long time, surrounded by glass, sky, and city lights.

"Okay." He kissed her nose and moved away. "Work it is, although fitting a ball gown on you won't be work. It will be a pleasure."

Eleanor's heart bumped and jittered. Did he expect her to strip down? She warred with that for a while. "May I see the design?"

"Not yet. I want to surprise you."

"You've already done that many times over."

He made the calls while they stood gazing out at the city. Taking her hand, he laced his fingers between hers without a word.

"I know you have a lot more questions," she said, "but I need you to trust me."

"I've never been intimate enough with a woman to truly trust her," he admitted. "But ... I do trust you. And I'm with you, no matter what. Remember that, Ellie."

"I'll try." Surprising herself, she curved into him and hugged him tight. "I promise I will."

A knock at the door pulled them apart. Eleanor tried to think ahead to all the scenarios playing out in her head, but one scene kept stealing the spotlight.

The scene where Nico held her in his arms and they danced the night away free and clear, flawed, but healed by each other. Her in a blue dress and him in a tuxedo. The world would melt away, and they'd forget everyone else in the room. That was the kind of dream that could scorch a woman's heart, and leave a permanent brand etched on her soul.

So Eleanor cleared her mind, waiting to be fitted by a man who knew how to please women. But a man who also knew how to break a woman's heart.

HER PHONE RANG early on Sunday. Before dawn.

Eleanor turned over in bed and stared at the number, but she didn't recognize it.

"Hello," she said sleepily, sitting up and running a hand through her hair.

"Hey, it's Annabelle."

Panic cleared out the cobwebs in Eleanor's head. "Annabelle, how did you get this number?"

"Johnny gave it to me," Annabelle said. "I'm in trouble, and he's in San Antonio for the weekend. He can't help me. And Aidan is AWOL, not answering his phone."

"What's wrong?" Eleanor asked, grabbing at her clothes. "Where are you?"

"I was at a party, and things got kind of crazy. Some people were arrested for disorderly conduct and noise violations. I'm cool since I was sitting in the backyard, but my scared date, who apparently has an outstanding warrant, took off in his Ferrari and left me stranded."

"Where is here?"

Annabelle sniffed, sounding as if she were trying to hide

she was upset, and then named a swanky address. "I'm out on the curb, waiting for a cab that never came. I guess I missed my last chance at a ride when I went to the bathroom. It's kinda cold out here."

Eleanor's throat grew dry. "Are you okay? You're not drunk, are you?"

"Not anymore."

"I'll be there in thirty minutes."

"Okay. Thank you."

Eleanor threw on some clothes. She was out the door in less than two minutes.

THREE HOURS LATER, Eleanor's phone rang again.

Nico.

She glanced at the guestroom where Annabelle was sleeping, and almost didn't answer. But she could use someone to talk to while she enjoyed the rest of the sunrise. "Nico? Hi."

"Hi. Would you like to meet me for breakfast?"

She would, but she shouldn't and couldn't.

"I can't. Annabelle's got into a bad situation, and I had to go and pick her up. She's asleep in the guestroom."

"I'm near your apartment," he said. "I'll bring breakfast to you."

"You don't need to do that, Nico."

"I'll be up soon."

Since Eleanor was still half asleep and hadn't had her second cup of coffee, she didn't argue. She quickly threw water on her face, brushed her teeth, and dabbed on some blush and lipstick.

Forty-five minutes later, a light knock sounded on her door. Eleanor hurried to open it, expecting fast food, but he'd gone to the grocery store instead.

"I can make a mean batch of pancakes," he said before kissing her on the cheek.

"You're too sweet," she said, thinking he had to have some flaws. "But pancakes sound pretty good."

Nico sat down the bags on the kitchen counter, and then tugged her close. "I missed you."

"How do you know where I live, and why did you just happen to be in my neighborhood?"

He laughed, the skin around his eyes crinkling. "You're scary when you're not quite awake."

"Well?"

"I have people who know people and … I wanted to see you again."

"You saw me last night, in nothing but a cotton slip, during the fitting."

"I enjoyed last night."

She smiled at that. "Me, too. Especially the part where your assistants placed cutouts on me, and pinned needles all along my spine and waistline."

"We have your measurements and the pattern. Now the real work begins."

"You didn't have to create a gown just for me, Nico. I would have taken something off the rack."

"No," he said, his eyes rich, dark, and yummy. "No. You

need an original one-of-kind gown."

"I shouldn't have brought you into this," she blurted, thinking it was way too early to be back in his arms.

"I'm interested in watching *this* play out," he replied. "You don't need to worry about me, all right?"

"All right."

"Let's cook breakfast," she said, hoping Annabelle would sleep a little longer. Whispering, she explained what had happened.

"She was just sitting on the curb?"

"Yes. Apparently, the man who brought her to the party left in a hurry to avoid the police. She was sitting in a swing alone in the dark when the police broke up the party, so they just told her to leave. I don't have the details, but I think she and her date had been fighting."

"Why didn't she call her mother?"

Eleanor gave him a hard stare. "Seriously?"

"Oh, right. The wrath of Caron."

"Yes. She called Johnny, but he took the weekend to see some friends in San Antonio. Aidan didn't answer her calls. Johnny told her to call me."

Eleanor understood Johnny's concerns, but he'd put her in an awkward position. Yet, she couldn't leave Annabelle on the curb.

"Maybe this will be a wakeup call for her to tone down her partying," Nico said. He chuckled. "Boy, do I sound old."

"You and me both. Caron's children seem a bit lost to me. As if they're just wandering in the wind."

"I talked to Annabelle at that soiree Caron and I attended last week," Nico said while he mixed flour, milk, and eggs. "I got the same impression." Slyly, he added, "You could be a calming influence for them."

Eleanor thought that over. "I didn't come here to babysit, but … yes, I suppose it couldn't hurt to show them a little bit of nurturing. They are on the payroll, but I don't think either of them is happy."

They were so involved in their conversation and each other that neither heard the bedroom door open.

"What's he doing here?"

Chapter Seventeen

ANNABELLE LOITERED IN the doorway, looking lost and forlorn in one of Eleanor's terrycloth robes.

"I'm making breakfast," Nico said. Shoving Eleanor's coffee into her hand, he said, "Why don't you two sit while I work my magic on these pancakes?"

Eleanor took Annabelle by the sleeve. "Sit. I'll make you some tea."

Annabelle frowned. "Are you two an item?"

"Yes," Nico said with a grin.

"No," Eleanor said with a warning frown at him.

"I'm going with the yes," Annabelle said. She rolled her eyes, waving her hand in the air. "Whatever."

Eleanor brought the tea, sinking down beside her on the couch. "How are you?"

"Better." Annabelle snuggled into the pink robe, looking every bit the lost little girl, her gaze taking in Eleanor's modest but modern apartment. "You have no idea. You saved me. The queen would not be happy about this at all. She accuses me daily of trying to make her look bad. I didn't have cab money, anyway, so thank you for picking me up."

Eleanor stayed quiet while Annabelle sipped the herbal tea. The girl kept her eyes down, picking nervously at a bird-embossed throw pillow. Annabelle's comments about her mother were upsetting, but Eleanor knew firsthand how cruel Caron could be.

"You needed help," she said, aware a handsome man was in her kitchen cooking breakfast. This whole morning was like a bad dream/good dream. It felt like she would wake up any moment.

"You won't go to my mother, will you?" Annabelle asked again, appearing young and afraid now that she'd had a shower and wore no makeup. Embarrassment made her porcelain skin blush pink. "And he won't either, right?" she asked, nodding her head toward Nico. "I'm an adult, but she still thinks I'm a child. This will only validate that mindset."

"No, we are not going to your mother," Eleanor said. "This never happened. You were never here. It's up to you how you handle whatever comes down the pike. But you might want to vet your boyfriends a little better."

Annabelle shook her head, her damp hair shimmering like black silk down her back. "I only had a couple of drinks. I'm not a big partier."

Eleanor shot Nico a glance before scrutinizing Annabelle. "Why do you present yourself as a rebel then, Annabelle? The punk boyfriends, the goth makeup and clothes, the implications that you're high most of the time?"

Annabelle shrugged. "I'm twenty-six and bored. I don't know what I want to do with my life."

"Do you like working at Castle's?"

Annabelle set down her teacup. "I did at first, but once I finished college, I thought the queen would actually let me get more involved. I wanted to help her and Mr. C with the company, but she kept trying to push me off on rich old dudes." She glanced toward Nico and made a face. "No offense."

"None taken," Nico said with a grin while he whipped the eggs to scramble. "I prefer someone a bit older. Around thirty at least." He winked at Eleanor.

Eleanor shot him another warning frown before turning back to Annabelle. "If you could have one job at Castle's, what would it be?"

"I love working with the displays and the seasonal décor," Annabelle admitted. "But ... I guess my ideas are too weird."

"What did you major in?" Eleanor asked.

"Interior design." Annabelle shook her head. "But that got me nowhere. My mother thinks I'm a loser. Lazy little Annabelle, she calls me."

Nico shook his head, anger clouding his face. Eleanor hid the rage coursing through her. How could a mother say that to her child? She wished she'd been a better older sister to Annabelle and Aidan, but she was here now. One day, she'd make that up to both of them.

"You need to assert your authority," she told Annabelle. "Not in a passive-aggressive way, but with confidence."

Annabelle did her infamous eye roll. "Right. Have you tried that with the queen?"

Nico brought them plates of fluffy pancakes covered with butter and syrup, with slices of fresh fruit and scrambled eggs. "As a matter of fact, she has stood up to the queen. I've seen her in action."

Annabelle stared down at her pancakes. "Forget it. I don't know where to start. The queen and I rarely speak to each other. I'm an embarrassment to her."

"You start by doing your best in the accessories department," Eleanor suggested. "Rearrange some displays. Create some interesting stories with jewelry, scarves, and purses, and then try getting to know your customers so you can help them look their best. See where that gets you."

Annabelle frowned, but then she smiled and cut into her pancakes. "You two are seriously weird."

"And so old," Nico said with another wink.

"Why are you with her, anyway?" Annabelle asked, just now catching up. "And don't try to deny it. You two have a thing. These pancakes weren't the only sizzle on that griddle."

"I was in the neighborhood, and had an urge to cook pancakes," Nico said. He left it at that.

"Right." Annabelle didn't look convinced. "Whatever. I was never here anyway."

"Right," Nico echoed, lips curling mischievously. "Now eat up."

"I think I'm done with the party crowd," Annabelle said. "People were just taking selfies and playing on their phones. Why don't people talk to each other anymore?"

"We're here," Eleanor said. "We can talk as long as you like."

Annabelle gave her a wane smile. "I need coffee."

"Coming right up," Nico said.

"You handled that with amazing clarity," Nico said later after they'd called a cab for Annabelle. Eleanor had wanted to give her a ride to the estate, but that would be too risky, so she'd paid for the cab with cash since Annabelle only had a charge card and some change.

"I've been there," Eleanor said, remembering her own wilder days. "Why do we become our worst while we're trying to get them to notice our best?"

"I don't have a clue," he said. "But I've certainly done my share of being at my worst. I've been at wild parties like that. And I've been bailed out of jail more times than I care to remember. Some of them, I don't remember. But once I hit thirty, staying up all night didn't seem as fun as it once was. Now if I stay up, it's usually work-related."

"Same here."

She wanted to hear all about his life, and she wanted to share hers. But she couldn't take that next step.

No matter how much she longed to blurt everything out, she'd come this far on her own and the less she revealed to him, the better off he'd be. Caron could bring down her wrath on his company, too, if she discovered Nico had been helping Eleanor.

No, better to wait until the big party. Hopefully before the end of the night, Eleanor could reveal herself to everyone. It would finally be over.

No more disguises, especially the one she'd used to close off her heart.

"I should go," he finally said, his gaze lingering on her with hints of wanting to stay.

"I need to get a shower and freshen up," she replied. "I want to check in with the weekend team to make sure the store is safe." She stared at her phone. "I should also call Annabelle and make sure she's okay."

"You are very dedicated."

"It's my job."

"I have a better idea," he said, slipping an arm around her. "I'll wait here for you to take a shower, then we'll go and do something fun together."

"I thought you had to get started on a very important dress?"

"I stayed up most of the night working on that. The seamstresses are probably sewing it together right now."

The man was an easy distraction. "What did you have in mind?"

"I want to ride out to the ranch," he said.

He was also good at surprising her. "Do I have to be the Lamon Lady?"

"Not today," he said. "Today, you can be you."

"Tell me about the place."

"My mother inherited it. It's been in her family for generations. She's a Texan, through and through. My father loved that about her, so they kept the ranch and visited it often in the early years. My family owns a place in Montana, too. That's mine now."

"Your parents were still close when he died?"

His gaze was shrouded in sadness. "Yes. She was with

him when he died. Their divorce couldn't stop the love they had for each other. They lived apart, but kept in touch."

"I'm sorry," Eleanor said. "Why did they divorce?"

"He was obsessed with work. Once he hit big, he became obsessed with having affairs with models and socialites. He made a lot of mistakes that cost him dearly."

Eleanor's heart hurt for Nico and his mother, but this made her understand him a bit more. "I'd like to get to know Lila," she said, meaning it. "She can't be all bad if she raised a son like you."

"But I was once all bad," he said with a raised brow.

"Not anymore," she said. "Not anymore, Nico."

"Go get dressed," he told her with a quick kiss. "We're going to the country."

Chapter Eighteen

NICO TOOK THE big SUV to the max as they headed toward Ft. Worth, but he kept glancing over to where Ellie sat in cowboy boots, jeans, a suede jacket, and a black sweater, with her hair in a ponytail and her skin fresh and sparkling. She looked young and carefree, her makeup minimal. Her attitude was relaxed, but hard to read.

He compared this Ellie to the woman who'd stunned that crowd at the fashion show. The same and yet different. Sophisticated and wholesome. Elegant and down to earth. Beautiful and sexy. Girl next door. A good person to call for help in the middle of the night.

He'd never been so confused about a woman in his life, nor had he pursued a woman in quite this way. Since he'd taken over the family business, Nico had poured his heart and soul into saving the House of Lamon. Being able to partnership with Castle Department Store was a big feather in his cap. If this Ellie was *the* Ellie, and Caron discovered them together, things could go badly very quickly.

But he wasn't worried about himself or Lamon. He was worried about Ellie.

"Are you okay with this?" he asked, nerves rocking along with the vehicle as they pulled up to the gates of the Double

L Ranch. He'd never brought a woman here before.

Was *he* okay with this?

"I'm fine," she said. "Just a lot on my mind. Other than going to church, I'm used to being lazy on Sundays, but this one has been kind of busy."

"What do you like to do when you're being lazy?"

"Sleep."

He could picture that. She'd be a sleeping beauty. Nico got an image of waking up to find her beside him each day, realizing he was in serious trouble. He'd only ever been serious about the House of Lamon, and even that had been forced on him. But now, he couldn't image his life any other way.

Except to have her in it. This Ellie. His Ellie. The woman in red, drenched in diamonds, and the woman in boots and jeans, drenched in suede. He wanted all the many Ellie's he'd met over the last few days.

But mostly, he wanted Eleanor Castle. The real woman behind the facade. But he wasn't sure if Eleanor Castle would ever come out from behind her protective mask.

"Are *you* okay with this?" she asked as he pulled the SUV up to the huge two-story house. He wondered if she'd just seen into his soul.

"Yes," he said, meaning it. "I was just daydreaming."

"About what?" she asked in a quiet, tentative voice, her gaze taking in the beige brick, aged stone, and the massive wooden columns that lined all the porches around the home.

"About you sleeping."

She blushed. "Not a pretty sight."

He smiled. "Does that make you uncomfortable?"

"No. Yes, maybe. It's been a while since I've thought about that kind of thing."

He got out and met her in front of the house. Then he tugged her close. "I'm not trying to seduce you, Ellie. I just needed to get away from the city."

"I know," she said. "I've got so much going on a break will do me good, too."

They entered the house, and he let her take it all in. The tiled hallway with the massive French doors to the backyard, with a pool clearly visible at the other side. The many spacious rooms on either side of the hallway, including his grandfather's study, a large den, and the wide kitchen and dining area.

She didn't speak for a couple of moments. Instead, she studied a pastoral portrait of the ranch centered over the fireplace. "I can see why you love this place."

"There is something about Texas," he said.

Her gaze moved over the room and then back to him. "I had an excellent job at a Castle store in a big mall, but … I knew what my heart wanted. I needed to come home to Texas."

Nico touched his hand on her arm. "I'm glad you did."

She turned to stare into his eyes. "This is amazing. No wonder you wanted to drive out here."

"Yes, I do love it here. My maternal grandparents, Nicholas and Helen Dawson, lived here. Back then it was called the Dawson Place. My mother later changed it to the Double L—for Lila Lamon. The house has been renovated and added onto over the years, but the bones are still good."

She took in the kitchen on one side, the huge dining room across from it that could seat up to sixteen. Both rooms, just like the den up front, had fireplaces.

"It has four bedrooms down the hallway," he said, pointing past the dining area. "Let me check things in here, and then we'll take a tour of the land. We own five hundred acres."

"That will be long tour," she said, her eye shining.

"More time with you," he replied.

AN HOUR LATER, they returned from riding horses across the back forty, laughing and talking about Texas and Nico's ancestors. He'd shown Ellie his favorite places on the ranch—the stream that flowed through it, the massive old oaks that graced certain corners of the pastures, the longhorns they were stocking now. There were so many things he'd missed by not being here full time.

Now they stood with the horses grazing by the stream. The sun was beginning to set off to the west over the pasture. He reached out to her, tugged her into his arms, and kissed her.

When they pulled apart, her eyes held longing tinged with regret.

"What?" he asked, wanting her to say what was on her mind.

"Nico, I'm worried about you getting involved in my

life."

He froze. "You don't want me in your life?"

"It's not that," she said, her eyes glistening. "I like you in my life, but ... this is all so mixed up. You don't need to be my hero. I can handle this, no matter what. But I have to try and make up for ... my past."

"Why don't you let me decide what I can handle?" he replied, hoping she'd finally come clean. "We seem to be doing all right so far, don't you think?"

"When we're together, we're great," she said, her fingers touching his jaw. "But we're going in different directions."

"Explain that, since we seem to be standing together right now."

"You've worked hard to obtain this huge account with Castle's. I don't want to jeopardize that. People who go against Caron Castle never win, but I'm going to do just that. I'm going to do something that could ruin things for you."

He took both the horses' reins, starting with Ellie back to the house. "I'm also used to taking care of myself, Ellie. You do what you need to do, and I'll worry about myself."

"But ... you don't know everything about me."

Turning the horses over to a ranch hand, he guided her toward the big porch that ran along the back of the house near the pool. "I know you use disguises to hide the real Ellie, and I know you love playing dress-up and wearing gorgeous shoes. I also know you loved wearing my Valentine shoes."

She gasped, her eyes full of surprise. "What are you talking about?"

"You're the woman in red—the real Lamon Lady you're pretending to be. But you're not ready to admit that or anything else to me. That's okay. I've figured out most of it. I'm telling you, I'm here for the duration. Until the end, Ellie. I want you to have a happy ending, but I also want you to be careful what you ask for."

She turned on the porch to stare out toward the descending sunset. "What do you mean?"

"Are you sure you'll be happy once you bring down Caron?"

Turning to face him, she said, "I'll be satisfied, Nico. Satisfied I'm doing what I should have done a long time ago. That has to be enough for now."

He nodded, but he didn't believe her. She was too kindhearted to be happy after sending someone to jail. She could regret that later.

"I know that feeling of wanting to turn back time," he said. "I arrived an hour before my father died, and even though I kept telling him I was sorry, I don't know if he understood."

Realization filled her eyes. "Nico, he knows. Look what you've done. You've worked so hard."

"Yes, out of guilt and a need to get past my father's betrayal. He'd caused my mother a lot of pain, but she forgave him. I don't know that I have forgiven him, though, even now."

Ellie stared at him. "Forgiveness is hard, but it comes when we're willing to forgive ourselves, too."

"But I can't go back to the past and change my actions or my father's."

"Are you trying to warn me to stop this investigation?"

"I won't interfere," he finally said. "But I'll be *here* when you decide you really need me, and when you're ready to be honest with me and yourself."

She didn't respond. Instead, she stood holding onto a square post, her head down. "That's why I don't think this is a good idea. I don't want you caught in the fray."

Nico touched his fingers to her cheek. "I was caught in the fray the night I placed those shoes on your feet, Ellie."

"Then you have to understand why I ran away."

"I do," he replied. "We can turn back, start over. Forget what I said. You're right; I shouldn't interfere."

Ellie inclined her head. "It's a little late to turn back now, don't you think? We both came back to Texas with our own goals. But I'm not sure either of us expected this."

"I didn't mean to hurt you."

"You didn't hurt me. Yet. I'm afraid you'll resent me if this plan of mine goes wrong."

"Really?" He brushed her hair away from her face. "I'm not going anywhere until I know you're okay. Until I know the real Ellie." He touched his forehead to hers. "We'll be okay, you and me. I promise."

She lifted away, her eyes misty and full of mystery. Then she kissed him. "I don't know if you'll be able to keep that promise."

As Nico drove the SUV away from the house, Eleanor studied the Double L ranch house, her heart hurting so badly she could barely breathe. Nico's warnings and wishes rushed through her head, making her feel as if she'd been running for a very long time and now she needed to stop.

This place held peace and quiet and a world of what-ifs.

She could imagine being here with Nico forever. Today had been wonderful, beautiful, an escape from the city and the world.

She didn't want to leave, but she couldn't stay.

"Do you want me to take you home?" Nico asked, his voice low and quiet.

She nodded. "I'm sorry if I overreacted back there." She faced him. "I told you I didn't want you involved, but you've managed to insert yourself in my life in a big way. I'm used to staying in the shadows, Nico. It's how I learned to survive."

His eyes held a jagged regret. "So I'm a complication? I forced you outside of your comfort zone."

"Yes. But … I'm the one complicating things for you."

"I told you I can handle my end. Caron would be foolish to renege on a signed contract, no matter what she thinks about you and I fraternizing."

"She won't like us becoming an item."

He finally smiled. "Is that what we're doing? Becoming an item?"

She leaned her head against the seat. "As I said, I don't know what I'm doing with you. I have a plan, Nico. I'm sticking to it. You have a plan that you need to stick with, too."

"Now that plan involves you, so I think we're even."

"You might change your mind on that once I give up this charade of being the Lamon Lady."

He shook his head. "I told you I'm not worried about that."

"I don't believe you'll give up your kingdom for me. That would be foolish."

"I've been known to be quite foolish."

"No, I won't let you do that," she said. "You want the woman in the red dress, Nico. But soon, you'll see the real me. You might not like what you see."

Spending time with him had been wonderful, like a dream, but she wouldn't bring him down with her. If she failed, she'd move on, knowing she tried. But she couldn't do that to Nico. He'd become caught up in her fight, in her drama. She had to stay away from the man and do what she'd set out to do.

What she'd been planning since the day she'd left Dallas.

WHILE THE LAST of the sunset covered the city in amber and bronze, Nico stood with Ellie at the door to her condo. "What can I do?"

"Forget about me once this is over," she said, turning toward the door.

"That's impossible," he told her. He pulled her back around and held her there. Then he kissed her with an urgency that conveyed his feelings. Lifting away, he said, "I can't forget the way you make me feel. I want to dress you from head to toe… and then undress you all over again."

She leaned her head against the door, her gaze studying his face. "You are a beautiful man and … you create beautiful things. We got caught up in a moment. Now that moment is over. There is no woman in red. There is only Ellie. Only me. I'm a security guard. I guard people and things, Nico. That's what I've trained myself to do."

"You guard your heart," he said, anger warring with the strong need to protect her. "That's what you're guarding the most."

"Maybe that's true," she replied, pushing away. "But it's mine to guard, and I'd be wise to remember that." Her features darkened in regret. "We both have obligations that can't be ignored. It's better this way."

Turning away, she unlocked the door and went inside, leaving Nico there with his bruised heart.

Chapter Nineteen

"I THOUGHT I'D check in with you. You've been awfully quiet this week."

Eleanor glanced to where Claude stood just inside the breakroom doorway. She'd been staring at the coffee pot for five minutes. Today, she wore her black wig again, her glasses pink and tinted, her suit denim and tailored. Floral-embroidered tennis shoes finished the look. But she really wanted to go back to being the wallflower she'd become when she left Dallas.

"I'm okay," she told her fatherly friend. "Just tired, and I've got a lot on my mind."

"You made it through your first week," Claude said, his chunky fingers holding his suspenders. "That's something, ain't it?"

"I've made a mess of my first week," Eleanor admitted. "Now I can't fix it."

"You'll get it figured out." He strolled over to the big bowl that always held wrapped snacks. "I'm hungry for a cupcake."

Eleanor laughed. "You used to bring me cupcakes from the chocolate counter."

"I'm pretty sure this one is fresh," he said, holding up a

red velvet one with candy hearts on top. "Want to share?"

"No, thank you. I pretty much worked my way through hundreds of cupcakes during college."

She wasn't hungry, and she still needed to fit into the dress Nico had designed for her. Mira had called her to say she should have the final fitting on Friday night at her apartment. An assistant would arrive with the dress.

An assistant, but not the man who'd created it.

Claude peeled the paper off the cupcake, and then took a bite. "Sweet." He winked at her. "Kid, you're doing the best that you can, remember that."

"What if I've been wrong all this time, Claude? What if I'm looking for the right outcome but for all the wrong reasons?"

"What kind of outcome do you expect?"

She shook her head. "I thought I wanted revenge. To bring Castle's back to its glory days. I had it all planned out. The exposure, the takeover, and setting things right."

"And now?"

"Now I don't know. I want to be a part of Castle's again. I want to do good things, expand, and keep our legacy going, but I'm not sure if I'm going about it the right way."

Claude munched on his cupcake. "Your father is a good man, but he was also ruthless when he needed to be. Fair to those he loved and to those who were loyal to him. What do you think he'd do if he found out someone he loves is siphoning off money to put into secret accounts and undermining employees to get them fired? What would he do with a person who turns her head when she knows a notorious shoplifting ring is working with someone inside her store?"

He rubbed his white beard. "She's collecting on insurance too much. It's why she had to save face and fire the last security guard. He turned his head for a pay-off. But she had to go with the board's vote on who became his replacement. This is no coincidence, princess. This is more of what goes around comes around."

Eleanor put her hands on her hips. "You're right. I have no choice." She'd come too far now, and she was so close. So very close.

Annabelle and Aidan walked into the breakroom, their expressions somber and the attitude of their united front tearing Eleanor apart.

"Hey, Claude," Aidan said, his laid-back swagger showing. "How's life?"

Claude chuckled and winked. "Life is always interesting. Sometimes the heart knows what the head can't figure out." With a smile at Eleanor, he headed back out to work.

"Why does he always talk in riddles?" Aidan asked before nabbing an apple.

"Why are you both here?" Eleanor asked, her pulse pumping a warning.

Annabelle pushed at her hair and grabbed a cookie. Her clothes and makeup were a bit more toned down today. She wore black jeans and a gray cashmere tunic, distressed scrunchy ankle boots, and chunky silver jewelry. Red lips.

"So … we know you're the lady who ran away with the shoes," she said without preamble. "Why did you do that, and what are you up to now?"

Not ready to have this conversation, Eleanor balked. "Did you mother send you two yet again to act as spies?"

"We don't talk to our mother," Aidan replied. "It's cool since Annabelle told me what you did for her. We're just curious. We sure aren't going to snitch." He grinned, tossed an apple into the air, and then caught it again. "This is way too much fun."

Eleanor couldn't trust them yet. "It's complicated."

"Wow." Aidan held up a hand. "That phrase is so last century. You saved my sister's skin and we wanted to thank you, but we need to understand what's really going on. Were you undercover that night?"

"Yes, I was," Eleanor said. "Very undercover. But I got caught up in the drama, and then I had to go after that shoplifter."

Aidan lowered his head and slanted a look at her, his dark bangs brushing over his eyebrows. "So you helped Johnny capture the thief that night?"

"Yes, I did. And that's all I'm going to say on that matter."

"Okay then," he replied. "We're with you. You helped with a shoplifter and you got my sister out of yet another disaster. Nothing to argue about there." He glanced at Annabelle. "I told you—you're too paranoid."

Annabelle fisted his arm. "Hey, I'm not that bad. I needed some answers. Now we have them."

"She's growing up so fast," Aidan quipped. He shrugged. "I have to get back to electronics. Those big televisions aren't going to sell themselves."

After Aidan left, Annabelle nibbled on her cookie. "Will you be at the Valentine's party at the house this weekend?"

Eleanor had to admire the woman's cool. "Yes. But I'll be on duty."

"Undercover again?"

"Very undercover again," Eleanor replied. She put down her empty coffee cup. On her way out, she said, "I hope I've covered all of your concerns."

"Most of them," Annabelle called after her.

Eleanor decided she might just stay *home* and *under the covers* that night.

NICO POURED HIMSELF into handling the needs of his impatient clients. The Lamon line was selling at top speed due to the ads they'd created. The mystery surrounding their spokesperson was trending on all social media outlets and most news stations. Today was Tuesday. Just a few more days and … everything would change. Then everyone would know the truth, too.

"Who is the Lamon Lady?"

"Where is she hiding?"

"Will she be revealed again at the annual Valentine's party at the vast estate of Charles and Caron Castle?"

"And why hasn't Charles Castle come forward? Just how ill is he, really?"

"Nico, what do you think of your new mysterious spokesperson? Was that whole *Cinderella running away with the shoes* your idea?"

All good questions. Nico refused to answer any. He was done, defeated, devastated. Tired. He'd finish up with the trunk shows and the press junkets all over town. After going out to the ranch for a few days to rest and recharge, he'd board a plane back to Italy and start the entire process over again in time for the fall collection that his employees were already working on.

Without his Ellie. Without Eleanor. Because she was so far undercover, she didn't know how to come out and be herself.

"Glum is not glamorous, you know."

He turned from straightening a display of spring dresses to find his mother staring at him. She wore a floral jacket and skirt, her bob shining like spun platinum. Her Lamon heels were made of soft turquoise leather.

"Hello, Mother."

"Don't 'hello, Mother' me," she retorted. "You've been acting rather strange. Does your mood have to do with that interesting security woman?"

Even his own mother didn't trust him. Could he blame her?

"That interesting security woman wants nothing to do with *me*."

Lila wagged a bejeweled finger. "Oh, no. That won't work. Or, as my father used to say, 'That dog don't hunt.'"

"Mother, what are you talking about? This isn't your concern."

But Lila was on a roll now, her eyes flashing fire, her

hands flapping in the air. "I've seen you two together. The day I met Ellie, you were about to kiss her right there in the lingerie department."

"We were in the hallway, and ... I wasn't about to kiss her."

"But you wanted to, didn't you?" Lila leaned close, her tone conspiring. "Caron Castle doesn't like how you're flirting with the help, but I don't mind one bit."

Nico gently escorted his mother to the café. "Let's get something to eat."

"Good idea," Lila said. "I'm famished, and the chicken salad here is to die for. You could use a good meal. Mira told me you've been working day and night on some secret project."

"Mira talks out of school. I should have fired her years ago."

"Mira loves you, and so do I. I came here to see you, but you resist me at every turn. I've been stuck with that crude Cruella de Vil all week."

Amused his always-above-reproach mother had Caron's number already, he kissed her on the cheek. "I'm sorry, I've been extremely busy since we've been here." He gave her a warning stare. "But do not gossip with Mrs. Castle about Ellie and me, okay?"

"I'm not here to gossip, and I ignore that dreadful woman's rants." Pointing to her left ear, she added, "In one side and out the other. But ... she does have it in for your Ellie for some reason."

Nico took that report under advisement. He'd have to

warn Ellie. If she'd quit avoiding him.

After they were seated in a quiet corner, he gave Lila his full attention. "So why are you so worried?"

"I had to see it for myself," Lila admitted.

"See what?"

"You with the woman who has finally captured your heart. Mira told me all about it. She thinks it's so romantic, but she pretends disdain."

"I'm definitely going to fire that woman."

"No, you will not. Mira sees things most of us miss."

"There is nothing to see, Mother. As Ellie put it, we had a moment, but now that moment's over."

"Oh, I think it's just beginning," Lila replied, her eyes on the menu. After they'd ordered, she patted Nico's hand. "You know I loved your father with all my heart, even after he *broke* my heart."

"Yes, I know that."

"Good, then stop letting his mistakes ruin your chances for love."

"Mother, you are giving me a headache."

"I'm trying to relieve your heartache," Lila said. She opened some crackers, and then buttered one in her dainty, ladylike way. "You're afraid to love because you think you'll be like your father, that you might have inherited his wandering eye."

"I've had my share of lustful romances, so isn't it obvious?" he snapped. "I won't do that to Ellie."

Lila put down her knife. "There it is. That passion and fire. I've never heard you talk that way about any woman until now."

"Yes, and my father talked about you that way, yet he betrayed you."

"I forgave that man seven times over," Lila said on a low whisper. "I loved him, but I had to leave him."

"I won't do that to her," Nico said, realization flooding over him. Ellie had pulled away, and this might be the real reason. "I want her, but not if she can't trust me. I won't hurt any woman the way he hurt you."

"You need to be you," Lila said on a motherly note. "Stop comparing yourself to him."

"Why didn't you ever tell me more about Dad? I had my suspicious, but … we never talked about it."

"As I said, I loved him. So I forgave him." Lila waved her hand in the air again. "I had to do what was best for the House of Lamon. That's the bottom line, always." She looked down at the gold-rimmed china. "You saw what happened when I finally did confront him. If I'd stayed—"

"He would have had that heart attack anyway," Nico finished. "He lived the good life a little too well." Taking her hand, he said, "It seems I'm not the only one holding onto to guilt over that man's peccadilloes."

"I miss him every day," Lila admitted. "But … you've done a wonderful job of keeping us afloat. You deserve some happiness, too, don't you think?"

Nico downed his mineral water before shaking his head. "You've got me. I'm in love. It hurts, I'm afraid, and she doesn't want to love me. End of story."

"No, not the end," Lila said. "The beginning. You've always been a fighter, Nico. Don't stop fighting now. Go after what you want. She's in love with you, but she's hurting, too."

"More than you'll ever know," he said, wishing he could tell his mother who Ellie really was. "And I don't think she's going to be honest with me about her feelings."

Lila chuckled, and bit into her cracker. "Just give me some time with her. My daddy had another saying. 'This ain't my first rodeo.'"

"Mother, no." Nico shook his head again, dreaded images shocking his mind. "Stay away from Ellie. You'll alienate her to the point that she'll never speak to me again."

"Then you'd better fix this," Lila replied in a calm voice, her silvery eyes full of steel. "If you don't, I will."

Frustrated, Nico spoke quickly to the waitress who had approached to take their order. "I'll have a steak sandwich, medium rare, with parmesan fries on the side. And … a beer."

His mother was right. He'd fix this. He wanted Ellie in his life, and he wouldn't have his mother running interference for him. He'd been ruthless in bringing Lamon back into the fashion forefront. He wouldn't let a beautiful, conflicted undercover blonde scare him away.

"You know, Grandfather had another saying."

"Oh, and what's that, darling?"

"Lock and load."

"Now your Texas is showing," Lila said with a wink. "This is going to be so delightful."

"I don't know about that," Nico said. "But it certainly won't be dull. By the time that Valentine's party is over, everyone in Texas will be talking."

Chapter Twenty

Eleanor saw Nico and his mother coming out of the café, so she turned in the other direction. She'd been trying to avoid him since Sunday. It was now Tuesday afternoon. The two longest days of her life.

But based on the hints Claude had dropped, she'd called in several employees who were willing to talk about the corruption Caron had been spearheading for years, and she'd managed to gather a lot more information. Enough to at least bring about an investigation into Caron's actions. Warrants would be served, and Caron would have some explaining to do.

But Eleanor was in a pickle about how to handle the whole thing.

What would her actions do to Aidan and Annabelle? She'd resented them when they'd come into her home and taken over her world. But they were young, confused, and … they'd moved from a modest house to what had to have looked like a real castle. Now, she could see it wasn't their fault their mother was cruel and conniving. Now she could see, in spite of Annabelle's own disguises and Aidan's cool withdrawal, they'd turned out to be pretty good kids. Adults now, she had to acknowledge. They both deserved a chance to succeed.

Would her actions against their mother set them back? She had everything in place. She'd consulted lawyers and met with local authorities, explaining her law enforcement background and her undercover status. The law made it very clear. With a solid case, Caron could go to jail for a long, long time.

There had to be a way to bring Caron to justice, while helping Aidan and Annabelle at the same time.

Tiffany found her heading back to her office with a pack of crackers and a bottle of water. "Is that lunch?"

"I'm not hungry."

"You said that yesterday."

"And I'm still not hungry today."

"C'mon," Tiffany said. "I brought leftovers from home. We can eat in the turret room. Smoked turkey and avocado sandwiches. My Wayne smoked that turkey on his cooker all day yesterday, and I sliced the avocadoes and tomatoes myself. I will be highly offended if you don't eat with me."

Eleanor gave a weak laugh, her eyes misting over. "I'll meet you up there."

She went up the hidden stairway and opened the side door to the old dressing room, memories assaulting her with each step. She used to hide on those stairs and wait for her parents to find her. This had been her secret room back then, and it had become her secret room now.

When Tiffany opened the door and came in, Eleanor forced a smile. "Do you always bring two sandwiches?"

"Sometimes I share with Claude, but he went out to

lunch with Johnny today."

"Those two are sure buddies."

"Yep. Claude knew Johnny when he worked here before. He's like a father figure to all of us, but he's especially close to Johnny. I think Johnny lost his parents when he was a teenager."

"That's horrible," Eleanor said, thinking she needed to get to know the whole staff better. She nibbled at the big sandwich. "This is good."

Tiffany chewed her own food. "So ... what's going on? Last week you smiled a lot. This week, not so much."

Eleanor put down her sandwich. "Nico kissed me."

Tiffany's mouth fell open. "What?"

"This weekend. And before, when we went for a walk in the park."

"You have been holding out," Tiffany said, a big grin covering her face. "So ... what now?"

"I don't know. Things were good, but then they went bad when I panicked. He cautioned me about what I was doing. He was right, and now I'm doubting myself and him. I'm miserable."

"Wait—" Her friend stared across at her. "Does he know who you are?"

"Not officially. He's guessing, but I'm not confirming. We're playing a game, speaking in vague code language, and tiptoeing all around the truth. He wants me to be honest with him. But ... I can't trust him enough. So ... he's hurt, and I believe he's afraid I'll regret what I'm planning on doing."

Wiping her hands, Tiffany said, "Oh, you mean that thing about revealing yourself at the big party, then telling everyone how our evil boss is embezzling and letting a shoplifting gang steal from Castle's, so they can profit on the black market? You mean that thing?"

She'd told Tiffany about her findings last night in a very quick phone conversation. Tiffany had suspected, but now they were getting close to the truth.

"Yes, that thing. I'm a mess. I don't know what to do."

Tiffany studied her for a moment. "You know, Eleanor, there are worse things than sending someone to prison."

"What could be worse than that?"

"Making them watch while you fix everything they've broken. Taking away what they claim to be theirs. If you can get that hidden money back, it would be a start."

Eleanor sat up, awareness flooding over her. "I see where you're going with this. I could come up with a slightly altered plan. But she will have to answer to several charges. I'd have to decide which charges I want to press, but the authorities might still go after her."

Tiffany chuckled and gave Eleanor a high-five. "She'll be the next Martha Stewart, living in a high-class jail cell."

Eleanor took another bite of her sandwich. "Now if I can just figure out how to get over Nico."

"I have a solution for that, too," Tiffany said in exasperation. "You don't get over him."

Eleanor looked out the window, remembering their first kiss and how they'd been together practically all weekend. "I won't have a problem with that. I'll never get over the man. I shouldn't have become involved with him in the first place."

"If you can't get over him, why try?" Tiffany said. "Let it happen, Eleanor. Let it happen the way it should happen. We all have obstacles in life, and you've overcome a lot of them. But … don't let being truly happy slip away because you're too caught up in a grudge to see what's going on in your heart."

"But it's not that simple," Eleanor replied, wishing it could be so easy. "I came here to win back Castle's, not fall in love with Nico Lamon."

"It's very simple. Either you fall in love and take your chances, or you go right back to being undercover and hiding your heart. And by then, it could be too late because Nico will be gone for good."

"He'll be gone anyway. I pushed him away because he sees the real me. I'm not used to being that intimate with a person. I've hidden myself away for so long I'm afraid to be truthful, afraid I'll lose him." Eleanor got up to pace around the room. "He has to go back to Italy, and I have to—"

"Stay here and hold down the store," Tiffany finished. "I get it. You have to do what you need to do. But … there has to be a compromise. Why can't you do both?"

Eleanor scoffed at that. "You mean take over Castle's and still be with Nico? How is that possible?"

"Nico has ties in Texas. His mother grew up here. He won't mind traveling back and forth."

"He doesn't have time to do that."

"Oh, I think he'd make the time," Tiffany said. "And you can go to Italy all you want."

"No. It won't work. Not if I'm here running things."

But remembering their time together at the Double L Ranch, she could imagine Nico spending more time in Dallas with her.

But she wouldn't ask that of him. It wouldn't be fair.

Eleanor paused, arms wrapped against her waist. "Life is full of twists, isn't it? I came home to help my father. Rushed in to save the day, all noble and self-righteous. And instead, I find a man who fascinates me, who looks like an Adonis, and ... who makes me feel like a princess all over again. But I was never a princess. I'm just a confused woman who's trying to capture something I lost long ago. I can't bring that back, and I can't move forward. Which do I choose, Tiffany?"

Tiffany rushed to Eleanor, and hugged her close. "You choose love, always, Eleanor. You choose love, even though sometimes it's the hardest choice."

Eleanor could see that now. Because she loved Castle Department Store. But she was in love with Nico Lamon.

NICO MOVED THROUGH the women's clothing department, glad his work here would finally be done. After the party Saturday night, this two-week promotional event would be over.

He wondered about Ellie. Would she keep shutting him out after what he'd said to her the other day at the ranch? He'd had all these grand plans, starting with taking her to the place he loved the most and ending with a big finale at the Valentine's party. But then he'd gone and messed things up by questioning her motives.

Why had he felt the need to advise her? He had no right to judge her for wanting to save Castle's. Hadn't he done the same thing?

It's because she can't be honest with you.

That voice inside his head came through loud and clear.

Nico had believed in his parent's marriage, had believed in romance and elegance and beauty. He'd followed his dad around like a little puppy, learning, listening, trying to emulate his father's every move.

Well, he'd done that all right. He'd become a playboy, a globe-trotter, spending too much money on things he didn't want or need. When Nico thought about it, he realized he'd never wanted to be a fashion mogul. He'd much rather stay here on the ranch. Learn to work the land and run cattle, the way his American grandfather had done.

What if he could do both?

He could still run the fashion house, but he didn't need to be in on the day-to-day designs. He'd trained several wonderful designers to help him rebuild the House of Lamon. Could he possibly pass the baton, but still be the boss?

He was so busy trying to figure out all the possibilities of that while he made notes on his cell phone that he didn't see the woman coming around the corner until he'd run smack into her.

"Oh."

Ellie. His Ellie. "I'm so sorry," he said, his arms automatically reaching for her. She smelled like fresh-blooming flowers. Was she wearing a Lamon scent? "Are you all right?"

"Yes," she replied, breathless. "I … I didn't see you there."

Nico focused on her, checking to make sure she wasn't shaken. "You're wearing pink glasses."

"Yes, and I don't think they're working."

"Well, they are rose colored," he quipped.

Adjusting them, she gave him that sultry-innocent stare that drove him a little crazy.

"Why are you in such a hurry?" he asked, wishing for time just to be with her.

She blinked, refocused. "I have things to do."

"We should talk. You'll still be my Lamon Lady at the party, right?"

She nodded, sadness clouding her eyes. "I have to be, yes."

"And you will still wear the blue dress?"

"Yes, of course. I'll pay you for your trouble."

"Ellie," he whispered. "Don't insult me. It's a gift."

She looked as if she *had* been thinking of him, at least. "Thank you, Nico. I have to go."

Turning, she headed in the direction she'd just come. Nico started to follow her, but no. She wasn't ready for that. He would wait until the party, and then he'd stand by her when she did whatever she planned to do. He'd have to prove to her that he wouldn't abandon her the way her own father had.

And then, he might just kidnap her and take her to his

ranch. Forever.

Or if nothing else, he'd corner her and make her see they belonged together and they could make this work.

Chapter Twenty-One

BY THE END of the day Friday, Eleanor had all of her facts straight and had built a strong case against Caron.

It would be easy to expose Caron at the party. After, Eleanor would have her removed from the premises. Missing reports, shady dealings with subpar vendors, and shell accounts that hid the truth. The accounting supervisor had been with the store for decades, but he was terrified of Caron and had listened to her veiled threats enough to do whatever she told him.

But he was even more terrified of going to jail.

Eleanor and Hank Pearson had come to an agreement. Eleanor would have to call the authorities, probably the FBI. The IRS would have to be called too, of course.

Hank had been scared, but then he seemed almost relieved. He'd be happy to testify. Yes, he had documented all of it, he assured her, because he was an honest man and hated what that woman had made him do.

Eleanor hated it, too. Too many employees had turned a blind eye to save their jobs because they had families to support. And because they remained loyal to Castle Department Store and her father. The security guard Eleanor had fired was nowhere to be found, so she figured he'd skipped the country.

But she had a convincing case.

Now she had the electronic files along with hard-copy reports. She planned to take everything to the FBI, knowing they'd want to do their own investigation. That could take months. Maybe years.

She had no choice. Once she presented her case, the authorities would take over the investigation.

After getting to know the employees and her stepsiblings, and listening to Tiffany and Claude's advice, she'd decided she'd confront Caron with a full backing of law enforcement.

They'd work out the details. If Caron didn't agree, Eleanor would prosecute her to the fullest extent of the law.

Would that be enough to save Castle's and her father?

Eleanor had to believe Caron planned to stick her father in an assisted-living facility and … just leave him there while she went through as much of his money as she could. Probably somewhere far, far away.

Sitting at the kitchen counter in her condo, Eleanor knew she might have another battle to fight once she'd confronted Caron. If her father had disowned her, what would she do then?

Eleanor had to do what she'd set out to do, regardless. She had to get to her father, make sure he was okay and help him in any way she could. He needed good doctors and proper examinations, not some physician Caron paid to come to the house.

But what if her father rejected her? What if he didn't want her help or didn't realize she was on his side? He might not even recognize her.

She prayed he'd know her and accept her back into his life. She'd been a coward before. She'd run away in fear and self-loathing instead of staying to fight for her father's love. Just like everyone at Castle's, she'd been too afraid to stand up to Caron.

Well, she wasn't afraid now.

I should have stayed and watched over him.

She'd do that this time, no matter what.

She might be in love with Nico, but her goal all along had been to return to Castle's and her father. Could she have both?

Tiffany had told her to choose love.

What else could she do? She loved her father.

As she sat here alone, she knew the answer was simple.

She had to fight for her father, but once she knew he was in good hands and as well as he could be, she'd also fight for Nico. Because she was in love with him.

And the first step would be getting into that house and to finally see her father face to face.

When her doorbell rang about an hour later, Eleanor glanced up at the clock. Seven.

She'd forgotten about the dress.

Today was the final fitting.

Surely Nico wouldn't be at her door? He'd said one of his assistants would bring the dress for her to try on.

She checked through the peephole to see Mira standing there. Wonderful. The woman glared at her each time they passed each other, and now she was going to help Eleanor with the dress?

But when she opened the door, she was surprised to see someone else standing with Mira in the hallway.

Lila, Nico's mother.

"Hello, Ellie. May I call you Ellie?"

"Mrs. Lamon, of course." Eleanor wanted to rush to the bathroom and put on some color, but it was too late to comb her hair or powder her nose. "Come in, please."

Mira gave her a once-over. "Will Tiffany be assisting with your hair and makeup tomorrow night?"

"Yes," Eleanor said, her spine stiffening. What exactly had Nico told these two?

"Good." Mira brushed past her with a white garment bag. "Your gown is ready. Mr. Lamon sent me personally to make sure it fits down to the last stitch. Eat only almonds and drink nothing but water tomorrow so you'll fit into it."

"Mira, honestly," Lila said, slapping a hand against Eleanor's wrist in a gentle comradery. "This woman is naturally beautiful." With a wink at Eleanor, she said, "You can eat whatever you want tomorrow. This isn't a beauty pageant."

Mira's frown defined aggravation. "Shall we get started?"

Lila took the garment bag. "If you need to slip on a robe, we'll wait."

"Yes, and I'll put up my hair, too."

Lila gave her an understanding smile. "Go ahead then."

Eleanor scooted into her bedroom and shut the door.

Why did his mother have to show up? Lila was a nice person. She reminded Eleanor of her own mother, which only made this even more bittersweet. Her plans were so intertwined with Nico's now she couldn't think straight.

After finding a clean robe, she thanked herself for wearing frilly underwear, and then opened the door to face what felt like a firing squad.

"Let's get this done," she said, her nerves jingling like Annabelle's bangle bracelets.

"I can't wait to see it," Lila said. She clapped her hands, a beautiful matron in a black pantsuit and pearls.

"There's a full-length mirror by the door," Eleanor said, noting Mira was carefully unzipping the garment bag. "My mother always had a mirror by the front door. That way, she could do a full-body check after she was completely dressed. The tradition stayed with me."

"You'll have to tell me all about your people," Lila replied. "Nico has been very mysterious regarding you, but he explained this dress is for undercover purposes. So mysterious."

Ah, so that's why his mother had come. A perfect opportunity to get the goods on the woman who'd been seen with her son. But Nico had set this up nicely, always the gentleman. "Yes, I'm afraid I do love fashionable clothes. And he was kind enough to design a gown for me."

Her mother would have liked Lila. She could imagine them heading to the country club to have tea together. "Not much to tell. Right now, I want to try on this gorgeous dress."

"Yes." Lila gave her another shrewd appraisal. "Mira, shall we?"

Mira finally smiled. "I must say, Nico has outdone himself. It's been a while since he's done such a hands-on project."

Lila's eyes, so like her son's, sparkled with interest. "He rarely designs clothes anymore. He's built quite a successful team for that, and he oversees them. He still enjoys designing shoes, though. And now this, and so quickly, too. He hasn't been this inspired in a long time."

She lifted the dress out of the bag, letting it fall across the back of the couch in all its glory while she watched Eleanor's face for a reaction.

Eleanor held her hands to her mouth to cover her awed gasp. "It's beautiful. I've never seen anything like it."

Lila nodded, her eyes on Eleanor. "Nor have I."

Feeling like a teenager again, Eleanor grinned. "Let's see."

Together, the women helped her put on the dress. After, they worked to zip it and fasten the pearl buttons that finished the back. Mira fluffed the skirt, allowing the swish of chiffon to whisper at Eleanor.

She turned toward the mirror, and stared at herself. "I can't believe this. It fits perfectly."

Lila trotted around the full chiffon skirt. She smiled. "Yes, a perfect fit. I can see that clearly now."

The dress was low-cut, but modest, with cap sleeves of lace and chiffon. The bodice held shimmering crystals that sparkled and winked their way down to the full skirt, a few of them moving like a waterfall down the folds of the luscious sky-blue chiffon.

"You'll need shoes," Mira said.

"I have a pair of Lamons," Eleanor admitted. "Silver satin, tall heels."

"They sound exactly perfect, too."

"Get them," Mira said. "Or tell me where they are and I'll bring them."

Eleanor laughed. "In my closet. Top right. Black box."

Mira giggled like a schoolgirl as she hurried away.

"Well, well," Lila said to Eleanor. "You've won over the toughest critic. She's the gatekeeper, you know."

"I do know," Eleanor said, wishing so many things. As she stared at herself in the mirror, her heart broke while the smile stayed on her face. "I don't deserve this. It's too beautiful. I'll never be able to repay Nico for ... his kindness."

"It will all work out," Lila said. "I have faith."

Eleanor couldn't speak. She wondered what Nico had told his mother, but she couldn't ask. She had no right to even hope.

"I have faith, too," she finally said, her throat tight with emotion. She'd have to take a leap of faith to get through the next few days.

Because she had nothing else left to cushion her fall.

Chapter Twenty-Two

HOURS LATER, AFTER hot tea and some chocolates Eleanor had found in the pantry, the two women left.

But they were both smiling when they exited the condo with the dress in tow.

"So tomorrow, you will report to Tiffany at the store," Mira said, having just confirmed that. "She'll get dressed there, too, so you can arrive at the estate together."

Eleanor couldn't disagree. The store would close early tomorrow, and the entire security team would be there to watch over the big event. The finale of Nico Lamon's two-week promotional extravaganza in the state where his father had fallen in love with Lila, and the celebration of a department store that had been a tradition in Texas for one hundred years.

The night should be a culmination of everything good and elegant and full of grace. Castle Department Store had always held those qualities. With Nico here, for a brief time, that goodness had returned. Eleanor was glad she'd been a part of the celebration but she would also be a part of a big scandal that could shut Castle's down forever.

Still conflicted the next day, she decided to go to the park and try to find the white pelicans. Would they still be there at White Lake?

Soon, she was in her little car, buzzing along while she tried to clear her mind of what lay ahead. Was she really going to dress up in that beautiful blue gown, go to the social event of the season being held in the home she loved, and try to spring her father?

Yes, she was going to do that somehow.

But now panic set in.

She could hold off on exposing Caron, and dance the night away with Nico instead. But she couldn't do that if she was supposed to be watching the crowd. And technically, Eleanor the security guard wasn't supposed to be dressed to the nines in a Nico Lamon original.

She'd created a big mess of her own making when she should just march into that party wearing her sensible suit, announce she'd caught the boss red-handed, and end it there.

But ... then she might not get to see her father.

Johnny was going to be on the lookout for the queen while Eleanor sneaked upstairs to find her father.

She'd asked Nico to help her get upstairs, but now she'd have to make sure to do that whenever Nico was occupied since she didn't want him involved more than he already was.

After parking her car, she slipped her cell phone into her pocket in case Tiffany called. They were going to meet in the turret room to get dressed together. Just like old times. Just the way they'd done two weeks ago before Eleanor's life had taken on a strange twist of déjà vu.

She began walking the perimeters of the big lake, searching for the white pelicans. When she looked across the water, she saw a flock gathered in the shallows. She hurried to the bend where she used to sit with her parents, her heart bursting with loneliness and memories.

But when she reached it, she came up short.

There on the bench sat a good-looking man with curly dark hair. When he turned toward Eleanor, her heart changed. It filled with joy and longing.

Nico had found the white pelicans, too.

HE STOOD, ALL of his prayers answered, and took in the sight of her. She'd taken down her hair, and tossed the pink-framed glasses. Today, she had on a red cashmere sweater, black wide-leg pants, and black boots. She looked so pretty his breath caught in his throat.

"Eleanor," he said, not even realizing he'd used her real name. "I was hoping I'd see you here."

"How did you know I'd be here?"

"I didn't," he replied while he tugged her to the bench. "I had hoped." Surveying her, he said, "And you're just *you* right now."

She caved. "Yes, I wanted to be just *me*. Before everything changes again."

"I like just you."

Sending him a confused glance while her pulse caught up with her heart, she watched the pelicans floating in the lake's cool waters. "This is my favorite spot. Aren't they so beautiful?"

"Yes," he said, sliding one arm over her shoulder. "I had to see for myself, but I agree."

"You called me Eleanor."

"Yes."

"You've known all along?"

"No. But after I saw you looking at the mural, I did a little research and figured it out." He glanced over at her, marveling in just her—the real Eleanor Castle. "I remembered something, too, while I was sitting here."

"Oh, what's that?"

"You, standing at an upstairs window all those years ago, staring down at me."

Eleanor twisted to face him, amazement on her features. "You saw me?"

He smiled. "I did. I don't know how I could have forgotten that princess in her tower."

"The princess who somehow got locked in the tower. I remember that day, too. I wanted to impress you, but I never got to meet you."

Grabbing her hand, he said, "Well, you've impressed me now."

She kept her eyes on the pelicans. "I had to come back, and I had to stay undercover. I'm so sorry I pushed you away, so sorry I couldn't be honest with you from the beginning."

"And tonight?"

"Tonight, I'll do what I came to do. I'm going to get my

father the help he needs, and I'm going to fire Caron Castle."

"And have her carted away?"

"I have a plan," she said. She turned to face him. "Will you let me see it through?"

Nico took her into his arms, his lips hovering near hers. "I'm all in, princess, whether you like it or not. I can't be a knight in shining armor, but I can be the man you need me to be."

He dipped his head to kiss her, savoring the taste of her, the feel of her, the heart of her.

Eleanor kissed him back as if it would be the last time, her heart and hurt filling him with the kind of need that made him want to fight dragons.

Pulling away, she stood. "I have to go and get ready. I'll see you tonight."

"I'll pick you up," he said, standing with her.

She backed away. "You don't need to do that."

"Eleanor, I'm taking you to the ball. What you do after that is your decision."

Because he didn't want to let her go, he rushed to her and held her close again. "We could leave right now. I'll get your father the help he needs. I'll get him out of that house and back with you. I'll handle Caron, too. We could just leave together, and you won't have to ever look back."

She seemed tempted, but regretfully touched her hand to his face. "I can't do that, Nico. I can't."

She stepped back another step, gave him one last sweet smile, and then turned and ran back up the path to the parking lot.

Nico had the feeling tonight might be the last time he would ever see her.

"YOU LOOK AMAZING."

Tiffany stood behind Eleanor while they stared into the standing mirror in the turret room, her smile saying it all.

Eleanor refused to get all emotional, but her soul seemed to be falling apart. "This dress makes me feel like Eleanor Castle again," she said. "I almost hate to wear it tonight."

"You have to wear it tonight," Tiffany said. "Nico will be out front waiting for you." Her friend's grin lit up her face. "And my Wayne will be picking me up, so we'll follow y'all."

Eleanor's nerves were trying to get the best of her, but she took a calming breath and studied her reflection. Her hair was upswept in a style that cascaded down her neck from a silver clasp. She wore solitaire diamonds on her ears.

She had on the silvery-gray Lamon shoes she'd worn the night she met Nico. The dress was fitted to perfection from the shoulders down to the waist, crystals sparkling like fireflies against the skirt that flared out in a flutter of gathered blue.

"I could be a white pelican, floating in the water."

"Pelican?" Tiffany shook her head. "No, baby, you're a swan. A beautiful swan."

Handing Eleanor her silver clutch, Tiffany checked the burgundy fitted dress she'd chosen. She touched a hand to her coiled braids, rubies shining in her ears. "Wayne is wearing a tux. Can you believe that?"

Eleanor smiled at her friend. "I hope you have a good time."

"How about you?" Tiffany asked. "Will you try to relax and have a good time before this big reveal goes down?"

"I'm about to change the whole landscape," Eleanor said. "I have to put a woman in jail or at least … expose her for what she is. I can't see the fun in that."

Tiffany's phone buzzed. "Wayne's waiting. Want to walk down together?"

"I think I'll wait here for Nico's call. I need a minute to myself."

"Okay. I'll see you there." Tiffany turned at the main door. "Eleanor, I know you. You'll do what's right. You're like your daddy. He always does the right thing."

"Thank you, Tiffany, for all of your help."

After she left, Eleanor sank down on the chaise lounge and stared out at the city. "I miss you, Daddy. And I miss Mother, always. I'm going to make things right. Tonight."

When she heard the side door opening, Eleanor expected to see Tiffany.

But the woman who pushed into the room wasn't her best friend.

"Hello, Eleanor," Caron said. "I think it's time we have a little chat."

NICO WAS OLD school. He didn't like texting a woman to let

her know he was outside waiting. Claude, who seemed to live at this store, let him in the employee entryway. Nico wanted to escort Eleanor down to the waiting car.

"Are you going to the big party?" he asked as they strolled toward the stairs.

"Nah, I hate these shindigs," Claude replied. "I'll probably hang with the night crew in security and watch the sports channel."

Nico would enjoy doing that, but he'd also much rather be with Eleanor. So he left Claude to go about his rounds, then headed for the dressing room on the top floor per Tiffany's instructions.

Checking his tux, he waited in anticipation to see Eleanor—Eleanor—in the gown he'd created for her. Then he knocked on the door.

And waited.

She didn't answer, so he called out. "Eleanor, it's Nico. I'm here to take Cinderella to the ball."

Nothing.

Nico knocked again. After a minute, he called on his cell. Her phone went to voicemail. His stomach burned with anxiety. "It's me. I'm standing outside. Where are you?"

Chapter Twenty-Three

SHE WAS STANDING among the crates, racks, and creepy mannequins that filled the old apartment that had once been part of her playhouse.

Eleanor glanced around, determined to find a weapon and a way out of here, her mind reeling. Caron stood in front of the door, laughing manically. Nico would be looking for her, but he wouldn't find her since Caron had locked the main door to the turret.

The same way she'd locked Eleanor's bedroom door all those years ago.

"No one will find you until Monday," Caron said coldly while she stalked around with a tiny pearl pistol in her hand. "And by then, you won't find me or your dear father. We'll both be somewhere far away, and no one will believe your twisted lies."

"I'm not the twisted one," Eleanor said, working to get past Caron. She'd have to use her wits, since her weapon was locked up tight in the security room and her phone was in the clutch Caron had knocked out of her hand earlier in the other room.

"Yes, you are," Caron said, her green dress bristling when she tried to walk. Her eyes were wild with anger and desperation. "I knew something was fishy when you walked into my office and immediately began with your 'holes in the security system' rant. I don't take kindly to be reprimanded in front of one of our top vendors. I started watching you then ... I had others watching you, too. When I saw you practically making out with Nico, I had my former security guard do some checking."

"That explains why I couldn't locate him," Eleanor said. "But I've got enough on you to make a few charges stick. I know all about your embezzling and the shoplifting ring. But for the life of me, I can't understand how you could do that to my father."

Caron hissed. "Shut up. You don't know what I've been through. He took ill after you left, whining day and night for his precious Eleanor and Vivian."

Knowing her father still cared gave Eleanor the strength she'd needed when she was a teenager. "So you decided to rob him and dope him up?"

"I'm doing what I need to do for my future. And for my children."

"Your children?" Eleanor swallowed back bile. Had her stepsiblings pulled one over on her yet again? She wouldn't shrink away this time.

"Whatever you think you know, Caron, is just the beginning. You're ruining Castle Department Store. This is the flagship store, and our profits are much lower than smaller stores in other cities. The Lamon account is saving us."

"Not my problem," Caron said. She leaned close. "You picked the wrong time to try and bring me down, missy.

You'd think you would have learned the first time you whined to your daddy about how mean I was."

"You're still mean," Eleanor told her. She lunged at Caron, ripping the other woman's dress at the sleeve.

But Caron twisted away. Eleanor held up her skirt and rushed the other woman, bending low to head-butt her right where her Spanx were the tightest. Caron went down with a grunt, her hand flailing and one of her shoes flying off.

Eleanor grabbed the gun, pointing it at her stepmother. "Don't move," she ordered as she rummaged to find some old curtain ties.

Her stepmother seethed, cursing, but she did as she'd been told. Crumpled on the floor, face twisted, she looked like a crazy person as she rambled about making Eleanor pay.

Once Eleanor found the ties, she made the woman flip over on her stomach and put her hands behind her back, ignoring her stepmother's rants. Eleanor quickly tied her hands, making sure the knot would hold. "This is how it's going to be, Caron. I'm going to the ball, and you're going to jail."

Turning, Eleanor Castle shot out the door lock. Escaping from this suffocating, musky room was the start of finally getting this witch away from her for good and reclaiming the life that had been stolen from her.

NICO HEARD A shot.

His stomach dropped. He whirled on the stairs and hurried back up, taking the service stairs the rest of the way to the top floor, heart pounding madly. Claude and a guard met him at the elevator.

"We heard gunfire," Claude said, wheezing, his bifocals falling down his nose.

"I did, too," Nico replied. "I was coming down to find you, since Eleanor didn't open the door or answer her phone."

"I don't like this," Claude said. "I know she hasn't left because I was watching for her. Wanted to see that dress."

Nico hurried along with them to the turret room, trying to keep his panic at bay. "Have you seen anyone else here tonight?" he asked Fred, the middle-age security guard with Claude.

Fred tugged at his gun. "Just Mrs. Castle."

"Caron?" Nico shot Claude a terrified glance. "Where was she headed?"

"Here," the guard said. "Top floor."

Nico tried the door of the turret room, his entire system going into overdrive. But before he could break through it, it flew open. Eleanor stood there in all of her glory, her gown flowing around her, hair falling out of its clasp in a riot of unruly curls, Her expression full of pride and triumph.

And she was holding a pearl-handled pistol.

"Call 9-1-1," she said, straightening her spine and touching a hand to her hair. "I'd like to make a citizen's arrest."

The guard did as she asked.

Nico frantically darted his gaze over her, searching for any injuries. When he didn't see any, he dragged her into his arms, kissing her in relief. When he broke away, he asked, "What happened?"

"I'll tell you in a minute," she said, holding him tight, "but first I want to make sure Caron is escorted to the police station."

AN HOUR LATER, Nico stood with Eleanor in the driveway of the Castle Estate.

"Are you sure you're ready for this?" he asked.

"Yes," she said, appearing confident. "I know what needs to be done. Let's get in there and do it. Tiffany and the others have stalled for us long enough."

He looked her over. "The dress held up well." He'd only needed to repair a few stitches. Raising a hand, he touched it to her hair. "I like this hairstyle better."

She'd hastily twisted it back up, capturing it with the silver clasp in an artfully messy upsweep. Her hair looked its best when she appeared to be running away. But tonight, she'd run into his arms. He hadn't let go of her since.

"Thank you. Ready?"

"Yes. You go to your father, and I'll mingle with the crowd until I find Annabelle and Aidan. After I escort them to a private room, I'll wait for you to join us."

"And no matter how that goes, we'll go back to the guests and … announce everything. Together." She smiled up at him. "It's not too late for you to stay uninvolved."

He grabbed her close to steal a kiss. "I told you, I am involved. With you. For a very long time."

Eleanor touched her hands to his face. "Let's go in then."

With that, Nico took her hand and guided her inside.

ELEANOR HELD HER breath. She'd called ahead to tell Tiffany what had happened. At this point, she couldn't be sure if her stepsiblings had gone to Caron, but she prayed they'd kept their promises. Tonight would be hard on them, no matter what they thought of their mother.

When they entered the main hallway, a collective gasp hit the crowd. Cameras began to flash, and Eleanor heard someone say, "That's her. That's the Lamon Lady."

Mira appeared, already well aware of what had happened, and gave them a nod. Lila was right behind her.

She took Eleanor in her arms. "Are you all right, darling? What a horrid thing to have happen."

"I'm fine," Eleanor said, searching for Tiffany, her gaze taking in the home she'd left so long ago.

Tonight, it was decked out in red, white, and silver, with giant Valentine's hearts hanging everywhere. Roses in beautiful vases were scattered across the reception tables.

Lila leaned in to whisper, "I had hoped you were *the* Eleanor. I remember her as a shy young girl then. But she's a force to be reckoned with now."

Eleanor blinked back tears. "Thank you."

Tiffany hurried across the elegant room to her side. "Everything is okay so far. I'm sorry I left you alone."

"I'm fine now," Eleanor assured her. "More than fine."

"Mr. Lamon, would you like to present your lovely new spokesperson?" a reporter called out.

"In a little bit," Nico said, moving through the crowd. But he looked back at Eleanor. "The Lamon Lady has to go upstairs to visit someone very special. She'll be back down very soon."

Tiffany guided Eleanor up the staircase. "The doctor you told me to call is on his way with an ambulance."

"Thank you. Is anyone with my father right now?"

"A nurse who's like a dang bulldog. But Wayne is taking care of that."

When they reached the second floor of the spacious Tudor-style house, Eleanor stopped and took a breath. "I can't believe I'm here again."

"I think your daddy has been waiting for you," Tiffany said. "Go on in. I'll be right here."

After hugging her friend, Eleanor straightened her dress before going in to see her father.

When she reached the big bed, tears flowed down her face. Her once strong, healthy father lay gaunt and quiet, his eyes closed. But he was alive. He was breathing.

"Daddy?" she said, taking his frail hand. "Daddy, it's me, Eleanor. I've come home."

Charles moaned, opening his eyes. Blinking, he stared up at her disbelievingly. "Ellie?"

Eleanor couldn't stop the tears. "Yes, it's me. I've come home, and I'm going to get you to a hospital, okay?"

"Eleanor," he said, grasping her hand. "I'm so glad you're

here."

"Me, too, Daddy. Me, too."

Eleanor kissed her daddy, not letting go of his hand until the paramedics came in to take him to the ER. After they'd checked his vitals and placed him on the gurney, she kissed him again. "I'll be there soon. Claude is meeting you at the hospital until I can get there, okay?"

"Claude. A good man. That's fine, honey."

Her father never once asked about Caron.

Eleanor followed the EMT team downstairs, and saw Nico waiting for her. She rushed into his arms. "He's okay for now. Let's take care of things here so I can go to the hospital. Claude is going to stay with him until I can get there."

"I'll go with you," Nico said. "Annabelle and Aidan are waiting in the study."

"What about the crowd?"

"Mira and Tiffany made the announcement. They promised a press conference first thing Monday morning. The reporters scrambled away with the scoop."

He hurried with her down a long hallway.

Eleanor took in the scents and sounds of her childhood home, remembering running down this hallway to find her father in his study. Now ... so much had changed.

When she entered the paneled room, she had to push away her emotions. Annabelle sat on a leather couch, dressed in a stunning white gown, her dark hair up with a tiny tiara crowning her head. Aidan wore a tailored tux, and he looked every bit the lord of the manor. She hated what she had to do.

Sinking down on an ottoman in front of Annabelle, Eleanor looked over at her. "I'm so sorry."

Annabelle's hurt expression said it all. "You should have told us."

"Yes, I should have, but I needed time."

"To accuse our mother and us?" Aidan asked, his anger measured with pain.

"Did you spy on me and report back to her?" Eleanor asked, needing to know.

"No," they both said at once.

Aidan paced the room. "She wanted us to do that, but ... we discussed it and ... we agreed that we somehow knew you. We spied only to try to figure things out. But we've learned to never give our mother any weapons to use against people."

"Did you finally figure it out?"

"No. Not until you came in tonight," Annabelle said. "Then it all made perfect sense." She gave Eleanor a hard stare. "Are you going to put us in jail, too?"

"No," Eleanor replied. "Of course not. I'm going to talk to the authorities, find out what will happen with your mother."

"But—"

"Earlier tonight, your mother held a gun on me and tried to lock me up. She admitted doing that same thing years ago when I was a teenager. She is in a lot of trouble, legally. I don't know what will happen. I'm sorry, but ... my father and Castle Department Store are my top priorities."

"And what has she done, exactly?" Aidan asked, his tone less hostile.

"Embezzlement, forgery, turning a blind eye to a shoplifting ring while she collected insurance money, just to name a few," Eleanor explained. "So she might be gone for a very long time."

Annabelle glanced at Aidan. "She's still our mother."

"Yes, she is," Eleanor said. "I didn't do this out of revenge, even though it started out that way. I did it for my father and for the legacy we were supposed to be celebrating tonight. If we can recoup some of the money she's hidden, I might be able to lessen the civil charges. But she's broken a lot of laws, and I can't help her on the criminal side. I hope you both understand."

"More than you'll ever know," Aidan said, pushing at his bangs. "But I'm going to the police station to see her. I need answers."

"Don't we all?" Annabelle added. "I'll go with you."

"I'll take you," Johnny Darrow said from the open door. "You don't need to do this alone."

IT WAS NEARLY midnight when Eleanor and Nico came back from the hospital. Her father was being weaned off the sedatives Caron's physician had been pumping through him. He'd make a full recovery. That was the good news. The bad news was he did have signs of early dementia, but with proper care and continued therapy, he should live a long time to come.

She'd get back to him in the morning after he'd rested. They had a lot to discuss. He might not like what she'd done to Caron, but she hoped he'd agree with her decision.

"Looks like the party is still going," Nico said, holding the door open for her. Soft music escaped into the night.

When they walked in, a crowd of mostly employees and board members merged together and applauded.

Eleanor stood in the middle of the estate house, taking in the people who now knew who she really was. She'd asked to come back here for the quiet, but now, seeing the dedicated people here, including Tiffany, Mira, Lila, and even Claude, she knew she'd done the right thing. Johnny came running in, obviously back from the police station. But she didn't see Annabelle or Aidan.

After hugs, drinks, and nibbling on what was left of the food, as well as dealing with reporters and photos, Nico came up behind her. He placed his hands on her waist to draw her back against him. "Do you want to stay here tonight or go back to your condo?"

Eleanor covered his hands with hers. "I'll need to go back there to change and get some things. Starting Monday, I'm going to clean this place up. Open it to the sunshine and fresh air. Same for the apartment at the store. Castle's is about to change in a big way."

He urged her around to face him. "Before I take you home, could you allow me one special favor?"

"What?" she asked. He was the most beautiful man she'd ever known, and he made her think of all of those fairy-tale dreams she'd held onto for so long.

"Will you dance with me?"

She nodded, unable to speak.

Nico took her into his arms. They swayed together to the music, waltzing through balloons, ribbons, and Valentine's decorations while everyone looked on and smiled.

He grinned down at her. "You know, you *are* the Lamon Lady. My Lamon Lady. What do you say we combine our efforts and make this work to our advantage?"

She drew back, lips curling slowly. "What do you have in mind?"

"Oh, about sixty years together, at least."

Her pulse did that heart-shaped flip. "Can we make that work?"

"Together, we can make anything work. You are an amazing woman, Eleanor. I love you. I want you. But mostly, I need you."

"I love you, I want you, and I need you, too," she repeated back.

His expression filled with joy. After he kissed her, he whispered, "Will you wear the red Valentine shoes to our wedding?"

"You know what they say," she murmured playfully, her heart expanding with happiness. "If the shoe fits …."

THE END

The Castles of Dallas Series

Castle Department Store is a downtown Dallas icon, but most of the elite shoppers who frequent the high-end store don't know the history of the beautiful mural in the shoe department. Come along with the Castle's to a world where glamorous high fashion and over-the-top romance brings about grand gestures and happily-ever-afters.

Book 1: *Undercover Princess*
Eleanor Castle's story

Book 2: *Rebel Princess*
Annabelle Castle's story

Available now at your favorite online retailer!

About the Author

Lenora Worth writes award-winning romance and romantic suspense for Love Inspired and also writes for Tule, Zondervan and Redbud Press. Three of her books finaled in the ACFW Carol Awards and several of her books have been RT Reviewer's Choice finalist. "Logan's Child" won the 1998 Best Love Inspired for RT. Her Love Inspired Suspense "Body of Evidence" became a NY Times Bestseller. Her novella in Mistletoe Kisses, along with several other writers, also made her a USA Today Bestselling author. With sixty books published and millions of books in print, she goes on adventures with her retired husband, Don. They have two grown children. Lenora enjoys reading, baking and shopping … especially shoe shopping.

Visit her website at www.LenoraWorth.com

Thank you for reading

Undercover Princess

If you enjoyed this book, you can find more from all our great authors at TulePublishing.com, or from your favorite online retailer.

Made in the USA
Coppell, TX
22 March 2023

14630950R00132